JUSTICE LEAGUE

Red Justice

JUSTICE LEAGUE

Red Justice

by

MICHAEL TEITELBAUM

Based on a story idea

by Keith Damron

BANTAM BOOKS
NEW YORK • TORONTO • LONDON • SYDNEY • AUCKLAND

RED JUSTICE

A Bantam Book/March 2003

Copyright © 2003 DC Comics. All rights reserved.
JUSTICE LEAGUE and all related titles, characters, and indicia are
trademarks of and © DC Comics.

ISBN: 0-553-48774-4

Visit us on the Web! www.randomhouse.com/kids
Educators and librarians, for a variety of teaching tools, visit us at
www.randomhouse.com/teachers

Visit DC Comics at www.dccomics.com

Published simultaneously in the United States and Canada

Bantam Books is an imprint of Random House Children's Books, a division of
Random House, Inc. BANTAM BOOKS and the rooster colophon are registered
trademarks of Random House, Inc. Bantam Books, New York.

PRINTED IN THE UNITED STATES OF AMERICA

OPM   10 9 8 7 6 5 4 3 2 1

For the writers and artists who brought the Flash/Barry Allen to life in the pages of DC Comics in the 1950s and '60s, firing my youthful imagination; and for a new generation of Flash fans: May Wally West speed his way into your heart just as quickly.

Special thanks to Keith Damron for the idea that set this novel in motion; Rich Fogel for his contributions to the tale; Bruce Timm and Warner Bros. Animation for the continuing high quality of the television episodes; Marissa Walsh of Random House for her input; Charlie Kochman of DC Comics for his usual good judgment, inspiration, and encouragement; and to Sheleigah, for reading the story first. —MT

PROLOGUE

Russia, 1979

Frozen mist swirled among gray clouds surrounding the towering Ural Mountains. Forming the border between Europe and Asia, Russia's Ural range stretched majestically for almost two thousand miles, rising to more than six thousand feet. Its broad brown shoulders covered in snowcapped peaks, the rugged range was home to one of Russia's largest industrial regions.

With the Cold War raging and the fall of the Soviet Union still more than a decade away, by the late 1970s Russia had concealed much of its chemical-, metal-, and machine-producing industries in the harsh environment of the Urals. There they would be safe from the view of the United States and its Western allies.

Many of Russia's weapons of war were forged in the factories nestled in these mountains.

Though certain secrets were kept even more hidden.

Deep beneath one of the tallest peaks in the central Urals, a large underground laboratory sprawled through caverns, some natural, others blasted out for the express purpose of creating this lab. The number of people who knew this facility existed could be counted on the fingers of one hand. Even the majority of Soviet military leaders were unaware that a top-secret experiment—designed to change the balance of power in the Cold War with the United States—was taking place beneath the grandeur of the famed mountain range.

The laboratory consisted of a large central area surrounded by several glassed-in control rooms filled with the latest in top-of-the-line Soviet technology. Across the cavernous central section from the control stations sat a huge steel door, twice as big as the largest bank vault, running from the floor of the cavern to its stalactite-covered roof.

The scientists of project Red Dawn had access to equipment that even the vaunted Soviet space program didn't know about. And they now hurried to put the finishing touches on the venture that had kept them occupied for the better part of three years.

The control room was a flurry of last-minute activity. Scientists hurriedly checked readings, jotting notes onto pads secured to clipboards. Technicians fed information into an experimental computer so sophisticated that no one except for the lead scientist on the project completely knew how it worked.

A short, broad-shouldered man in a military uniform entered the main control room, striding confidently. His thinning black hair peeked out from beneath his standard-issue Soviet Army cap, and the long line of shining medals on his chest told of decades of loyal service to the Soviet people. But nothing he had done in his storied military career compared with the importance of the experiment whose final touches he had come to oversee.

"Good evening, General," said one scientist, standing at the arrival of the imposing figure before him.

"Resume your work!" the general barked. "We've got a deadline to meet."

"Yes, sir," the scientist replied, quickly inputting information into the computer.

Leaning on the edge of a control panel, the general peered through a wall of thick double glass into the lab's central room. There he saw five figures lying on their backs on gleaming steel tables, thick metal restraining straps across their chests and legs. The entire control room was bathed in eerie red light, pulsating as it washed over each of the five bodies.

Glancing down at his watch, the general sighed, then looked back into the central room, rubbing his chin anxiously. *I'm getting too old for this,* he thought, just as a tall, thin man with red hair and a gray-speckled goatee stepped up beside him. The man's long white lab coat was wrinkled, and it looked as if he hadn't removed it in weeks.

"Ah, General Kolnikov," he said, extending his right hand. "You're early."

"Actually, Dr. Pushkin," the general replied brusquely, grasping the scientist's hand in his own. "*I'm* right on time. You're *late.*"

"Yes, of course," Dr. Pushkin said, glancing over the shoulders of the technicians seated in front of him, checking their work. "The precision of the Soviet military."

Pushkin was the lead scientist on project Red Dawn. Although the idea had come from the general, it was Pushkin's genius that had taken the concept from theory to reality. His knowledge of the latest computer systems, coupled with his skill in genetic engineering, made him the perfect choice to lead the scientific team. Which is why, as project director, General Kolnikov had picked him, even though the two didn't always see eye to eye.

"Are you sure this is necessary?" Kolnikov asked impatiently, gesturing to the procedure taking place before them. The general respected Dr. Pushkin's abilities, although as a military man he often regarded scientists as necessary evils in the interest of national security. In this case, science was the key to gaining the upper hand if a war between the Soviet Union and the United States ever did truly come to pass.

"Absolutely, General," Pushkin replied. "Those going through cryogenic freezing must be exposed to this stabilizing field immediately before the freezing process and soon after awakening, in order to maintain the integrity of their genetic structures."

"Fine, fine," the general said impatiently. "Spare me the technical details and just get on with it!"

A few seconds later, the brilliant red lights flooding the control room shut off, replaced by a dim white glow lining the walls. The restraining straps on each lab table retracted, freeing their occupant. Five figures swung their legs around into seated positions, then slid from the tables, moving slowly across the shadows.

General Kolnikov squinted through the glass, staring as the five stepped robotically toward the massive steel door on the far side of the room. In the lead walked a tall, barrel-chested man with bulging muscles rippling along the length of his body. He was followed by a slender, graceful woman with flaming red hair that reached down to her narrow shoulders. Then came a being that appeared to be half man, half bird, tall and thin with huge wings, long legs, and a sharp beak. Behind him walked a short, powerful-looking woman, as wide as she was tall, built of solid muscle. A trim man in a tight-fitting yellow bodysuit brought up the rear. His forehead glowed with a radiant yellow aura.

As the strange group approached the vault door, it swung open silently, revealing an empty room lined with gleaming white walls, like the inside of a giant refrigerator. Without hesitation the five figures walked into the room; then the mammoth door swung shut.

"This is it," said Dr. Pushkin, punching in a sequence on his keypad. "Three years of hard work, all coming down to this."

"Skip the big buildup, Doctor," Kolnikov replied. "I know the significance of this moment. I don't need any extra dramatics."

"Very well, General," Pushkin said; then he pressed a button on the control panel.

A loud hiss filled the laboratory, accompanying frosty vapors that poured from tiny vents in the vault's door. When the icy mist cleared, the door was sealed.

"Well?" Kolnikov asked nervously.

Pushkin checked several gauges, then turned to the general. "The subjects have been successfully placed into cryogenic freeze," he announced, smiling broadly. "And their life signs are all stable. They are in perfect hibernation, and will only be revived at your command. Congratulations, General. Your project is a success."

General Kolnikov allowed himself a satisfied grin and a sigh of relief. He nodded tersely toward Pushkin and turned to leave.

"Oh, General," Pushkin began, pointing to his private office. "May I have a quick word with you?"

Kolnikov grunted his agreement and followed Pushkin into a small closet of an office, closing the door behind him.

"General, I have something of great importance to show you," Pushkin began, remaining standing. "I'm certain it will be of interest to you. It's in another lab I have set up not far from here."

"Another lab?" Kolnikov challenged. "Why do I not know about this?"

"It's a private facility," Pushkin explained, shrugging casually. "For my own personal research."

"Personal research?" the general repeated, scoffing at the implication. "Doctor, this is the Soviet Union. What belongs to you, belongs to me, and certainly belongs to the Soviet military!"

"Which is why I'm choosing to show it to you," Pushkin said calmly. "Please, come with me."

Rubbing his leathery face with a thick-fingered hand, General Kolnikov followed Dr. Pushkin from his office, through the control room, then into an elevator, which rose quickly to the parking level of the hidden facility. Climbing into Dr. Pushkin's sports car, the two men raced toward what appeared to be a solid wall of rock.

Pushkin pressed a button on his car's dashboard and a section of rock slid up, revealing a curved opening in the wall. Exiting the secret facility, the tiny sports car zoomed into the wintry late afternoon.

"This better be worth it, Doctor," Kolnikov said, squirming in his seat. "Maybe you should slow down."

"I'm fine," Dr. Pushkin replied as the car sped along a narrow, snow-covered mountain road. "I've driven this route thousands of times."

With the lightweight car slipping and sliding, Dr. Pushkin struggled to stay in control. On their left the majestic mountain rose into the clouds. To their right, the road dropped off to a sheer cliff that vanished into the gathering darkness below. Snow fell gently from a slate gray sky, and Pushkin squinted through the tiny windshield as his wipers tossed the freshly fallen powder aside.

Winding along the twisting, turning road for a few miles, the two men finally approached an outcropping of rock. The overhanging shelf formed a natural garage into which Pushkin pulled his car. As he stepped out, the doctor pressed a button on a tiny handheld device that he pulled from his pocket. The mountain face before them parted, opening into a narrow doorway.

"Nice trick," the general said, following Pushkin into the mountain.

"Thanks," replied the doctor as the door slid closed behind them. He pulled out a flashlight and led the way down a damp, narrow tunnel. "A little ingenuity, a little expertise."

"A lot of money," Kolnikov added. "No wonder Red Dawn was over budget."

The two men followed the flashlight beam through a series of branching tunnels. The last tunnel led into a small room. Pressing a knob on the wall, Pushkin turned on the lights. Kolnikov was surprised to see a miniature version of the lab he had just left. A small control room packed with equipment led to a tiny central area. The general spotted a door across the main room that looked like a smaller copy of the door leading to the cryogenic freezing chamber at the other lab.

"I'm getting déjà vu," the general said, glancing around.

"Yes, it is quite similar to our main facility," Pushkin replied. "I had this one built first and tried out some early freezing experiments."

"So what did you bring me here for?" Kolnikov asked.

"Right this way," Pushkin replied, throwing a switch on the control panel and pointing to the large vault door that now swung open slowly.

General Kolnikov looked across the room, peering into the freezing chamber. This too looked like a miniature model of the one that now contained the five frozen figures.

Without warning, Dr. Pushkin pulled a blackjack from his coat pocket and struck Kolnikov across the back of his head. The general blacked out, collapsing to the floor in a heap.

Slowly, Pushkin dragged Kolnikov's heavy, limp body across the room, toward the open doorway of the freezing chamber.

When he was halfway inside the vault, Kolnikov regained consciousness. He reached back out, grabbing the door handle for balance, struggling to keep himself from being pulled all the way into the chamber.

"Have you lost your mind, Pushkin?" he shouted, trying desperately to scramble to his feet.

"No!" Pushkin cried, shoving the general back down. "With you out of the way, I will gain complete control of the unlimited power of Red Dawn!"

Kolnikov, a career soldier, was surprised at the strength of his wiry adversary. That, coupled with his weakened condition from the blow, made his struggle for survival an exhausting effort.

"Why not just shoot me?" he asked, reaching up and grabbing Pushkin's arms.

"I may need you someday, if Red Dawn proves too much for me to control," Pushkin revealed as he grappled with Kolnikov. "That is why I have chosen to freeze you!"

The door to the chamber slammed shut. Already programmed into the control panel by Dr. Pushkin, the freezing process automatically commenced, filling the central area with icy mist.

A single furtive figure slipped silently from the secret facility. Wending back through the branching tunnels, he stepped out into the snowy night. Slipping into the waiting sports car, he then sped out onto the narrow mountain roads.

On the drive back to the main lab, Dr. Pushkin's car slid awkwardly on the slippery road surface, which by this time was covered with a thin coating of snow and ice. As the lightweight vehicle hit a sharp curve, it skidded, spinning out of control.

Flying off the road, the car plunged into the chasm far below, exploding in a ferocious fireball as snowflakes drifted gently toward the blazing wreckage.

CHAPTER

1

Present day

The Flash sped through the streets of Central City. At the edge of his field of vision, buildings and sidewalks blurred and smeared like colors smudged across a newly painted canvas.

Ahead he caught sight of a two-year-old girl plunging from the tenth story of an apartment building. Speeding up slightly, Flash caught the child in his arms.

"Gotcha, sweetheart," he said, smiling, as the startled girl stared up at him, not knowing whether to cry from the shock of falling or laugh at the funny man in the red mask.

Flash dashed up the ten flights of stairs to the girl's apartment and handed her over to her grateful mother. "Better get some safety bars on that window," he said. Then he vanished in a streak of crimson.

Speeding around a corner, Flash felt the world bending at its edges again. He spotted a thick column of smoke rising from an office building up the street. Reaching the base of the structure, he circled it again and again. People looking on appeared to be frozen in the space between one second of time and the next, as the Flash increased his speed with each pass.

The spinning motion of his rapid circles created a whirlwind, which rose along the outside of the building. The powerful gust of wind quickly blew out the flames.

Nearby, a bank robbery was in progress. Two thieves had managed to tunnel into the bank's vault. The robbers had dug their way in, taken the money, and were about to slip back out through their tunnel.

The Flash streaked up to the vault's heavy steel door and stopped before a group of anxious bank employees. Focusing his concentration, he vibrated the molecules in his body. To the onlookers, he appeared like a fuzzy video image that suddenly vanished— seemingly right into the door. Flash felt the individual molecules that made up his body blend with, then move past, those of the steel door. Passing through the thick layers of metal, he emerged on the other side, inside the sealed vault.

The robbers, reacting as if they were seeing a ghost, dropped the sacks of cash and headed for their tunnel. Reaching the entrance first, Flash unleashed a powerful blow to each of their jaws, flattening the thieves.

He grabbed the first robber, then leapt into the tunnel, speeding along its rough-cut floor, emerging three blocks away through an open manhole. Streaking back to the bank, he dashed through the front door, then dropped the robber's limp, unconscious body at the feet of the bank manager.

"Did you order a criminal?" he asked the amazed man, who stared at him with his jaw gaping wide. "Or was it the tuna on whole wheat? I forget." Before the stunned manager could speak, Flash repeated his journey in reverse—back to the manhole, through the tunnel, up into the vault, then back again—returning with the other robber in tow. "And here's dessert!"

Streaking from the bank, Flash looked up and suddenly found himself on the wide-open salt flats of Utah. An endless expanse of white butted up against the horizon in all directions. Moving at top speed, he felt as if he could run forever.

Slow, a voice in his mind said. *Slow down.*

Aware of each stride, Flash forced himself to slow the pace of his dash. He shifted from speeding along as the Fastest Man Alive to running like a top Olympic sprinter.

Slower still, said the voice, soft but firm.

Flash slid into an easy jog, then a slow trot, then finally a walk. A feeling of calm and control washed over him.

Then unexpectedly, in the blink of eye, he blasted back to his top speed, a blinding red blur against the pristine white sand.

"I'm sorry, J'onn," said Flash, opening his eyes. "It's just not working." He was, in fact, not in Utah. Nor had he just saved a falling child, put out a fire, or foiled a bank robbery.

The Scarlet Speedster was sitting in the lotus position—his legs crossed beneath him, his hands resting on his knees—on a soft mat in a dimly lit room on board the Justice League's orbiting headquarters known as the Watchtower. His Justice League teammate J'onn J'onzz, the Martian Manhunter, floated in midair beside Flash, also in the lotus position.

Leaping to his feet in frustration, Flash paced back

and forth across the narrow room. "I'm trying, J'onn," he said, shaking his head. "But it's really hard!"

"As is everything worth learning," replied J'onn. The green-skinned native of Mars drifted slowly to the floor, extending his legs, landing gently on his feet. He had been trying for weeks to teach Flash meditation and relaxation techniques. Being a telepath, J'onn had projected his thoughts directly into Flash's mind as a soothing voice. Flash then used the imagery of his physical speed to try to control his zooming thought processes.

"You sound like my high school guidance counselor," Flash snapped back harshly. Thrilled to be the Fastest Man Alive, Wally West, the youngest member of the Justice League, suffered from a side effect of the accident that had given him his great speed. Wally's mind raced along in accelerated time. He constantly felt frustrated and impatient in dealing with normal humans. To him, they seemed incredibly slow, almost as if they were moving and speaking at half speed.

Wally found it nearly impossible to stay focused on one train of thought, no matter how interested in a conversation he might be. As soon as someone began speaking, his brain took off in ten different directions at once. This was often mistaken for disinterest or just plain rudeness, but it was nothing that he could control. And so he had come to J'onn J'onzz for help in slowing things down a bit.

"I'm sorry, J'onn," Flash said as he continued to pace. "I didn't mean to snap at you." He had thought that working on meditation and relaxation techniques was a good plan when J'onn first suggested it. But now, after weeks of struggle with minimal success, he was no longer sure.

"I understand," J'onn said calmly. "You are working to control your very nature. Something we all struggle with from time to time."

"Yeah, but, you're like 'Mister Calm' all the time," Flash said, stopping long enough to look directly at J'onn. "And besides, if you get bored with a conversation, you can just turn semitransparent and drop down through the floor."

"Speaking of such things," J'onn replied, "I noticed in that last thought sequence you imagined yourself passing though solid steel. Is this really physically possible for you?"

"The last man to wear this costume could do it," Flash said, referring to Barry Allen, the previous Flash and Wally's mentor. "I've been practicing, but I haven't quite gotten the hang of it yet. But since it was my fantasy I figured, what the heck, why not do it there?"

"Shall we resume?" J'onn asked.

Flash shook his head as he reached for the door. "I can't do any more today," he said, frustration clear in his voice. "I'm too wired. And besides, I've got a date tonight. I'm heading home. Thanks, J'onn. See ya."

Opening the door to the tiny room, Flash sped through the twisting corridors of the Watchtower. Arriving at the launching bay, he glanced through a window, looking down at the Earth below. Then he boarded the *Javelin-7*—the Justice League's own space shuttle—and slipped into the pilot's seat. Easing the ship from its docking port, Flash fired its main engines and punched in a course for home.

The sleek spacecraft—a smaller version of the shuttle used by NASA—was available to any Justice League member for transport to or from Earth. Most of those who used the *Javelin-7* just locked in its autopilot for the short trip. But the Flash simply could not sit still long enough to enjoy an automated journey. He checked the ship's navigation readouts, fuel indicator, and engine condition, knowing exactly what the gauges would say—they were the same each time—but it gave him something to do.

Grabbing the piloting controls, he steered the vessel toward North America, preferring to fly the ship himself. "Ah," he sighed as the bright blue globe grew larger in the cockpit window. "The glamorous life of a super hero."

CHAPTER 2

Wally West stepped out of the shower and snatched a towel from a hook on the back of his bathroom door. When he was not busy being a super hero, Wally lived in a small studio apartment in downtown Central City. As usual he was between jobs, and with next month's rent coming due, he was banking on the job interview he had scheduled for the next morning.

Wally had as much trouble holding down a job as he did keeping friends. His constantly active mind and its resulting short attention span usually got in the way. It prevented him from taking the time to thoroughly learn a new job before his boss ran out of patience and fired him.

Add to that all the time he devoted to his life as the Flash, and he became even less of a candidate for Employee of the Month. As Wally dried himself off and slipped into a bathrobe, his mind was not on tomorrow's interview, however. He was anticipating the date he had tonight with Linda Park.

Wally was looking forward to seeing Linda again. The two had met at a party in his neighbor's apartment the previous week and had seemed to hit it off during their short conversation. Having a mind that raced along at hyperspeed was a mixed blessing. His short attention span led to problems on most of his dates: dilemmas like remaining interested in what the person he was with was talking about for more than a few seconds.

Wally viewed himself as a popular, likeable, friendly guy, and so he was troubled by the fact that most of his social encounters ended in disaster. On the other hand, the same short attention span that led to these problems also prevented him from dwelling on his failures for any length of time; he approached each new conversation with supreme confidence, his past disappointments long forgotten.

With a carefree jaunt in his step and a song from the latest Remy Zero album on his stereo, Wally West headed for his closet to choose the clothes he was going to wear that evening.

Which is when the doorbell rang.

Huh? Wally thought. *Who could that be? Linda isn't due to show up until seven, and it's only . . .* He glanced at the clock on his night table. It read 7:03. *Seven oh three! Yikes! I lost track of the time.*

The doorbell rang again.

"Who's there?" he called out, knowing full well who was there.

"It's Ed McMahon," came a sweet female voice from the other side of the door. "You've just won the Publishers Clearing House Sweepstakes!"

Wally smiled, despite his awkward situation. He had liked Linda's sense of humor the moment he'd met her.

"Come on in," he said. "Door's unlocked."

As the doorknob started to turn, Wally dashed back into the bathroom, slapped water and shaving cream onto his face, then swiped it off with his razor. Wiping his face clean, he splashed on his favorite aftershave. Zipping to his closet, he yanked his clothes from their hangers and onto his body in one swift motion. Then, running a comb through his hair with his left hand, he changed the CD in his stereo to something a bit more mellow with his right. Finally, he picked up the magazines and newspapers scattered around the place, piling them neatly in the corner.

All this before the doorknob finished turning and the door to his apartment swung open. In the doorway stood a pretty young woman with short brown hair and large green eyes. She was wearing a black skirt and a long-sleeved black blouse.

"Hey, Linda," he said, smiling, gesturing for her to come in. "Right on time."

Linda Park had been looking forward to seeing Wally again. Although they hadn't talked for very long at the party, she was drawn to his quick wit, bright smile, and sense of self-confidence. She entered and joined him near the small kitchen area.

"Nice place," she said politely, glancing around at the thrift shop furniture that lined the tiny box of an apartment, and the concert posters that covered most of the walls.

"Hey, it's not much," Wally replied, pulling a couple of glasses from a kitchen shelf. "But I like to call it . . . small. Still, I'm just waiting for that big break, and then I'm out of here."

He opened the fridge and pulled out a bottle of iced tea. "Cold drink?" he offered.

"Sure," Linda replied. "Big break, huh? So, what is it that you do?"

"Me?" he answered, filling both glasses, then handing her one. "I'm an executive administrative assistant coordinator."

"In other words," she began, pausing to take a sip, "you're unemployed."

"Bingo!" he replied, pointing at her as if she had just won a prize. "But I've got an interview tomorrow, so I'm practically out of this palace.

"Hungry?" he asked, quickly changing the subject away from his own pitiful financial state.

"You bet," she replied, finishing her tea and noticing that Wally's glass was empty, though she never saw him take a sip. "Starved."

"Excellent," Wally said, putting down his glass. "There's a new Mexican place on Second Avenue. They've got outrageous burritos."

"Burritos it is, then," Linda agreed, placing her glass on the narrow kitchen counter. Then she turned and headed toward the door.

Snatching up his keys, Wally followed, excited,

thinking that he really liked her. This time, things would be different.

At Bandito's Mexican Hacienda, Wally and Linda found a table near the window. Conversation flowed easily at first, moving from topics like recent movies, new music, and the fact that finding an affordable place to live in Central City was getting harder and harder.

Wally talked a bit about some of the many different jobs he'd recently held, and how he really hoped to settle into a career he could stick with. The most important part of his life, however—his career as the Flash—remained a subject that was off-limits to Linda and everyone else he met. This fact only added to his feelings of loneliness.

"So tell me what *you* do?" Wally asked when he had finally stopped talking about himself. He settled back to listen. As in the past, that's when things started to go bad.

"I'm a freelance photographer," Linda explained. "I work for a couple of magazines, sometimes sell my stuff to newspapers. And I've got a proposal in with a children's publisher for a book about baby animals, and—"

By the time Linda had reached the part about her

book proposal, Wally's mind had already veered off in five different directions.

I really like her, I hope I can stay focused long enough to—

Hey, I never noticed that painting before. They used to have one of a bullfighter and a—

I still can't believe J'onn spends all his time at the Watchtower. He should get out in the world, like me. He always—

If I don't get that job tomorrow, I'm going to have to do another tap dance for my landlord so I don't get—

I wonder when tickets to the Smash Mouth concert go on sale. Last time I waited too long and—

A small voice from somewhere in the distance filtered its way through Wally's cascading thoughts. "Wally?" he thought he heard it say. Then again "Wally?" This time a bit louder.

Then finally, "Wally West!" a booming, angry voice shouted, shattering his private little world.

Wally pried his mind free of its speeding train of thought in time to see Linda Park stand up from the table. She practically knocked over their waiter, who was bringing their two supergiant burritos, as she turned to leave.

"I've been shouting your name at you for five

minutes," she said angrily. "As soon as the conversation turned away from you, it was like I was talking to a blank wall. If you're not interested in what I have to say, then why did you ask me out? Enjoy your burrito. In fact, enjoy both of them. I'm outta here." Then she stormed from the restaurant, vanishing into the crowd on Second Avenue.

Wally stared out the window after her. *No,* he thought. *This time it was not any better. Different woman, same ending.* Tossing a few dollars onto the table, he picked up both burritos and walked from the restaurant, heading for home.

Once again, the mixed blessing of his short attention span prevented Wally from dwelling on this latest failure for too long. As he wolfed down both burritos, though, he noticed that the pain of rejection lingered a bit longer than usual this time.

He was still feeling hurt and sad when he reached his apartment. Flopping onto his bed, he grabbed the remote to his stereo, switching on the CD he had started earlier.

Could J'onn's meditation techniques actually be a mixed blessing as well? he thought as the first crunching guitar chords poured from his speakers. *Could the attempts at slowing down my thinking also force me to dwell on the disappointment? Those techniques certainly didn't help me tonight. Linda was really nice, and smart, and funny. She had no way of knowing that I wasn't being intentionally rude.*

Maybe one day J'onn's lessons can help me feel normal during a conversation. But I doubt it.

As Wally struggled with these questions, the tiny comm link in his left ear—a communications device worn by all members of the Justice League—beeped wildly.

Emergency!

The thought quickly blocked out all others. Wally West leapt from his bed and donned his Flash costume in the blink of an eye. Then he tore from his apartment in a streaking crimson blur.

CHAPTER 3

"This is a bad one," said Green Lantern's voice through Flash's comm link as the Scarlet Speedster headed for a remote spot in the rural suburbs just outside Central City. He was on his way to a small clearing in a large wooded area. Whenever he needed to summon the *Javelin-7* to pick him up via remote control, he guided the ship to this secluded spot. He now figured he would need to meet his teammates on the Watchtower.

"Talk to me, pal," Flash replied as the city faded from view and he turned onto a small country road.

"An earthquake in Russia is causing a possible meltdown in one of their oldest nuclear power plants," Green Lantern explained. "The Pavlovich

Nuclear Energy Facility in the Ural Mountains. The Russian authorities contacted Washington, and J'onn got a call at the Watchtower."

"Russia!" Flash exclaimed. "It's Chernobyl all over again."

"Worse," Green Lantern reported. "This one's so old, the aftershocks could send the whole place tumbling. The Russians have no way to stop a potential meltdown. Our government could help, but by the time they mobilized and transported the equipment they would need, it would be too late. If the core melts down completely, the resulting explosion and radiation could mean the deaths of millions."

"Enter the Justice League!" Flash said, arriving at the familiar clearing. "First on the scene at any disaster."

"You got it, hotshot," Green Lantern replied. "No one else could get there fast enough. Superman, Wonder Woman, Hawkgirl, and I are on our way to the Urals right now. I'll send a signal through your comm link. You should be able to track us and follow on foot, but chances are you'll get there first."

"I'll save you a seat," Flash quipped. "I'm on my way."

Abandoning his plan to summon the *Javelin-7*, the Flash streaked from the clearing, heading east.

In the sky over the Atlantic Ocean, four costume-clad figures flew as fast as they could above the churning blue swells and whitecaps. Superman sped along in the lead, followed by Green Lantern, Wonder Woman, and Hawkgirl, communicating with each other via comm link.

"We're going to have to stabilize the containment area around the radioactive core," Green Lantern explained as he zoomed along, surrounded by a green aura radiating from his power ring. John Stewart took his responsibility as a member of the Green Lantern Corps very seriously. He also felt a strong commitment to the other members of the Justice League.

"There's also the building itself and the surrounding structures," Superman pointed out, scanning the skies ahead with his telescopic vision for any low-flying aircraft that might cross their path. "They'll have to be shored up against the aftershocks." His famous red cape rippled in the wind behind him as the Man of Steel tried to work out details of an impromptu rescue plan in his head.

"I understand that the reactor is located in a remote part of Russia," Wonder Woman stated. Since deciding to reside in the world of mortals, Diana, Princess of the Amazons, had been learning as much as she could about their planet. "At least it is not in a densely populated area."

"That's little comfort," said Hawkgirl. "When one of these nuclear reactors go, the wind can carry the radiation for hundreds of miles. Within hours it could reach millions of people."

"Then we'd better hurry," Green Lantern said, increasing his speed. "I sent a signal to Flash. He should be able to find us by—"

"By looking for costumed people flying above the Atlantic Ocean?" said a voice from below, finishing Green Lantern's statement. "I passed three or four other groups on the way, but there's no mistaking your lovely emerald glow, GL."

Looking down, Green Lantern spotted Flash running on top of the water. "Cute, hotshot," the Emerald Warrior replied. "Glad you could make it. Now, take the lead and let us know what you find."

The Flash was back in action, moving at top speed. This was where he felt most comfortable. All thoughts of his disastrous date and, in fact, his entire life as Wally West faded along with the eastern coastline of the United States.

Flash's legs pumped furiously. As one foot slapped the surface of the ocean, giving him a millisecond's worth of traction, the Flash brought his other foot forward, repeating the move. With each step, the surface tension of the water supported his weight just long enough for him to shift his balance to the opposite foot. As long as he kept moving, he could remain on top of the water—and moving was what he did best.

Within seconds he had passed Superman, and was now on track to arrive in Russia first.

"Do we have a plan?" Flash asked as the blinding movement of his feet created a wake on each side of his speeding body.

"Somewhat," Green Lantern explained. "We've got two or three main objectives."

"Right, objectives," Flash repeated, already unable to muster the focus needed to absorb all the details he felt were sure to follow. "I knew that."

Green Lantern shook his head. He appreciated Flash's talent and courage, but he wished that the young hero would grow up. That seemed to be about the only thing he didn't do quickly.

"I'm just about to hit the coast of France," Flash announced, spotting a vague stretch of land in the distance.

Reaching Europe, the Flash dashed across the countryside of France, then passed through Germany, Poland, and Belarus before finally entering Russia. In each country, he left puzzled people staring after a fierce gust of wind and a blazing red blur sweeping by.

After a few more minutes, the Flash arrived at the rugged Ural Mountains. "I've reached the foothills of the Urals," Flash reported. "Now what?"

"According to the information I received, the nuclear facility should be about two hundred miles to the north," Green Lantern replied.

"On my way," Flash said.

Speeding the last two hundred miles along the mountains' twisting, turning roads in a matter of seconds, the Flash arrived at the Pavlovich Nuclear Energy Facility.

"This looks really bad," he reported as he dashed around the power plant, assessing the situation. The towering nuclear reactor rose before him. Shaped like a large round porcelain coffee mug, the huge structure trembled as the ground shook from the earthquake's repeated aftershocks. Small cracks emerged along the side of the reactor, and pieces of the structure crumbled to the ground. "It doesn't look like the reactor is going to hold up under all the shaking!"

Before any of the Flash's teammates could respond, Superman arrived, landing beside the Scarlet Speedster.

"You weren't exaggerating," the Man of Steel said, taking in the scene of chaos and destruction. He quickly scanned the facility with his X-ray vision. In addition to the main reactor, he spied ten buildings sprawled across the enormous complex. They housed offices, communications facilities, and technical equipment used to power, cool, and control the reactor.

They were also filled with terrified people.

The buildings shook and cracked as more aftershocks struck. Television news crews captured the panic and pandemonium on video, putting themselves at considerable risk just being near the unstable reactor.

"Superman is here with me, GL," Flash said,

watching as people fled from the buildings. "I think we need your plan—objectives and all!"

"Right here, hotshot," Green Lantern replied, not through his comm link, but as he landed beside the Flash and Superman.

Before Green Lantern could say another word, a stout, gray-haired man in a long white lab coat came running frantically from one of the technical build-ings. "Heroes from the West!" the man cried, racing toward the Justice Leaguers. "Thank you. You must help us!"

"That's why we're here," Green Lantern replied. Chunks of concrete and glass split from the nearby buildings, tumbling to the ground, crashing among the facility's fleeing employees.

Wonder Woman landed, followed a few moments later by Hawkgirl.

"Flash," Green Lantern began. "Use your speed to carry as many of those people to safety as possible. Hawkgirl, see what you can do about those falling chunks of the buildings with your mace."

Without a word, Hawkgirl flapped her huge wings and sped toward the buildings.

"I'll help you," said Superman, taking to the air.

Flash streaked toward the ten buildings, each of which shook and shattered from the powerful aftershocks. Hysterical people poured from the doorways, shrieking with fear. Added to the threat of a nuclear meltdown, they now had the immediate problem of escaping from their crumbling offices.

Moving at an incomprehensible pace, the Scarlet Speedster raced up to two people who were running from a building, just as a large piece of concrete plunged toward their heads. Grabbing one person in each arm, Flash carried them away as the deadly mass crashed to the ground with explosive impact.

"You should be okay here," Flash said, placing the shaken couple a safe distance away. Then he turned and zoomed back to the disintegrating structures, racing toward two more fleeing employees.

Meanwhile, Hawkgirl moved swiftly through the air, riding the wind currents with her great wings spread wide. Again and again she swung her energy-enhanced mace. Sizzling bolts of jagged white power crackled all around the heavy black weapon as each swing connected with a falling chunk from the buildings.

WHOOM!

Hawkgirl's power-laced weapon vaporized the dangerous debris, turning it to dust and smoke, which showered down harmlessly upon the escaping people.

Superman flew from building to building, catching pieces of the falling facades before they struck the panicked crowd. He then tossed the bulky chunks aside, where they landed a safe distance away.

Between the pieces that Hawkgirl pulverized and the ones Superman redirected, many of the deadly projectiles were stopped from causing any harm.

Reaching two more people, Flash repeated his task, carrying them swiftly to safety. Again and again he raced back, darting through the tumbling debris, removing others from harm's way.

At the same time, cracks spread along the top portion of the reactor itself, expanding in a spiderweb pattern. Green Lantern and Wonder Woman flew quickly toward the splintering structure.

"If that reactor tower crumbles, the containment chamber that holds the radioactive material will split apart and we'll have a meltdown for sure," the Emerald Warrior explained.

"I'll try to stabilize it with my Golden Lasso," Wonder Woman announced, pulling the tightly coiled, glittering rope from her belt.

"Great!" Green Lantern shouted. "I'm going to work

on getting inside to check on the condition of the containment chamber."

Unfurling her magic rope, Wonder Woman formed a large loop. Tossing the glowing circle high into the air, she guided its descent as it drifted down over two sections of the splitting tower. When the rope dropped below the spreading cracks, the Amazon Princess yanked hard, pulling the loop tight with her enormous strength.

This added support shored up the splintering tower, cinching the structure with its magical force, preventing the deterioration from going any farther. Hovering in midair, Wonder Woman strained, her fists clenched tightly, adding her power to that of the rope.

She silently prayed to the gods of the Amazons that her strength, along with the meager structural support that remained from the reactor's initial construction, would be enough.

"Hang on, Diana," Green Lantern yelled, seeing the strain on Wonder Woman's face. "I'm going to cut a small opening through the reactor wall and slip inside to check the containment chamber!"

A thin green beam shot from the Emerald Warrior's power ring, striking near the base of the trembling structure. Using the powerful energy strand like a blowtorch, Green Lantern slowly sliced through the reactor's thick outer wall.

Completing a two-foot-high cut, he turned the power beam at a right angle and started a horizontal line. Green Lantern grew frustrated by the slow progress his ring made through the dense cement, hoping he could finish cutting open a section big enough to slip though before the whole thing collapsed.

Suddenly the section of the reactor above Wonder Woman's lasso began to crumble. Small pieces from the top of the tower chipped away, tumbling down around Green Lantern's feet. As he finished his horizontal cut, the Emerald Warrior realized that he would not have enough time to complete his task before the tower came down. The containment field would break down, and nuclear disaster would follow.

CHAPTER 4

Green Lantern shut down his narrow power beam. "I didn't make it in!" he shouted up to Wonder Woman. As Diana maintained her taught grip on the rope, she swerved in midair to avoid the increasingly large chunks of the reactor falling all around her. "I'm going to create a force field with my ring to help you hold the reactor together!"

"Any assistance would be greatly appreciated," Wonder Woman replied, straining mightily as the structure continued losing its integrity.

A wide green swath expanded from Green Lantern's power ring, rising until it covered the entire reactor. With the tower shored up by the force field, the pieces of masonry stopped falling. "It seems to be working," he shouted.

"I can tell," Wonder Woman replied. "Holding these cracking pieces together got easier the moment you surrounded it."

"Problem now is, there's no way to know what shape the containment chamber is in," the Emerald Warrior worried. "It doesn't matter how firm this outer wall is. If that inner chamber breaks open, we'll have a major meltdown on our hands."

"I've got an idea," a deep voice called out from behind Green Lantern. Peering over his shoulder, he spotted Superman hovering in the air behind him.

The Man of Steel had been keeping an eye on the situation at the reactor, while deflecting the falling pieces of the other buildings. Peering through the reactor's outer wall with his X-ray vision, Superman found the containment chamber, deep within. "The chamber is beginning to crack," he reported. "I think I can get inside and repair it with my heat vision."

"How?" Green Lantern wondered. "If I let my force field down to cut an opening, the whole thing could topple. And you can't just smash your way in—you'd destroy the containment chamber!"

"Not if I approach it from underneath!" Superman replied.

The Man of Steel rose into the air, then began flying down toward the ground, his body perfectly straight, his powerful arms extended. Bringing his hands together, Superman started spinning like a giant drill. His fingertips formed a diamond-hard point, which cracked into the ground, opening a hole.

Down he flew, spinning and digging a narrow tunnel. When he had gone deep enough, Superman shifted direction, angling toward the reactor. Tunneling in a straight line, the Man of Steel carved through the earth, using his X-ray vision to guide him to a spot beneath the containment chamber.

Superman first tore through solid rock, then burst through the metal base of the reactor. There he found himself staring at the core's containment chamber. Large cracks continued to spread along its thick walls. Then a tiny hole opened, releasing powerful radioactive energy.

This is in worse shape than when I first looked at it just minutes ago, Superman thought as a sickly yellow glow washed over him. Aiming his heat vision, he sent intense beams of red-hot energy sizzling along the cracks. Some of the smaller ones sealed up, but when the twin beams from Superman's eyes reached the hole, it only widened further.

It's no use. I can't seal the hole!

Flying quickly back though the tunnel he had created, the Man of Steel emerged beside Green Lantern and reported his bad news.

"The containment chamber is too badly damaged," he explained.

The strain started to show on the Emerald Warrior's face. "That means this thing could blow any minute," Green Lantern said. "I think my force field can contain and even absorb the radiation, but the force of the blast would topple buildings for miles."

"Then we've got to get the entire reactor away from here!" Superman concluded. "John, can you open a small section in your force field just big enough to let me through?"

"You got it," Green Lantern replied. Adjusting the force field emanating from his ring, the Emerald Warrior created a narrow opening at the base of the reactor. Superman slipped through this gap, which then sealed shut behind him.

Now surrounded by the force field, the Man of Steel grasped the base of the reactor firmly. Setting his feet, he lifted with his powerful arms, veins bulging in his neck from the effort. The towering structure moved a fraction of an inch. Superman drew a deep breath, then made a second attempt to hoist it from its base. The reactor didn't budge.

"I'm going to need some help here," Superman admitted, adjusting his grip for another try.

"I'll give you a hand," said Wonder Woman, "if Green Lantern's force field will hold without my lasso."

"We have to try," the Emerald Warrior stated, exhaustion creeping into his voice. "I think I can keep the reactor together without your rope long enough for us to break it free. At least, I hope so!"

Wonder Woman slowly loosened her lasso's grip on the top section of the reactor. Quickly coiling the rope, she hooked it onto her waist. Slipping through a small opening created by Green Lantern, the Amazon Princess swiftly entered the force field.

She took up a position on the opposite side of the reactor from Superman and gripped the tower's base, adding her enormous strength to his. Together they heaved straight up, their muscles straining to their limits. This was, after all, a permanent facility. The engineers who had built it forty years earlier had never envisioned a time when it might have to be removed from its base.

Lifting together, Superman and Wonder Woman managed to tear the reactor free.

"Thanks, Diana," the Man of Steel said, adjusting his grip, taking the full weight of the tower onto his shoulders.

"I'll go check to see if Flash and Hawkgirl need any help," Wonder Woman announced. Passing back out of the force field, Diana flew toward the crumbling buildings.

"Let's get this thing as far from Earth as we can," Green Lantern shouted, maintaining his force field, which now contained not only the reactor, but Superman as well.

"Agreed," replied the Man of Steel. "Let's go!"

Superman dug his fingers into the smooth concrete of the reactor's outer wall. With his grip secure, he took to the sky, flying straight up, bearing the weight of the massive tower. Green Lantern flew alongside, keeping his force field in place.

As the two heroes vanished into the sky, Wonder Woman reached Hawkgirl. The winged hero from the planet Thanagar continued smashing chunks of the falling debris. Nearby, the Flash dropped two people off a safe distance from the buildings, then dashed back in for two more.

Wonder Woman followed him into a building, which teetered on the verge of collapse. "I've got these two," she said, grabbing the terrified employees around the waist, carrying them to safety.

"Get bored working with the big boys, Princess?" Flash asked as he streaked away with two more people in tow. "Decided to join the 'B' team?"

Their friendship had gotten off to a somewhat rocky beginning, thanks to Flash's self-important view and slick-talking approach to meeting new women. But in the months they had spent working as part of a team, Wonder Woman had come to respect the Scarlet Speedster and had even begun to appreciate his somewhat warped sense of humor.

"I believe I can be of some assistance," she replied.

"Hey, you can work a disaster at my side any day, Diana," Flash quipped. "There are only a few more folks to get out of this building. The others have all been evacuated."

Just then a loud sizzling noise caught Wonder Woman's attention. Whirling around toward the spot where the reactor had stood, she saw a dozen electric cables waving in the air, sparking wildly, writhing like frenzied snakes. The power lines had been severed when the reactor was ripped from its base. They now protruded into the air, whipping back and forth out of control, sending jagged plumes of electricity cascading in all directions.

Racing back, Wonder Woman unfurled her Golden Lasso. Ducking and dodging the snapping cables, she tossed her magic rope, catching a few wires at a time, until she had managed to gather all of the flailing cables together.

Surging jolts of electric power traveled along the length of the lasso, sending repeated shocks into Diana's body. Grimacing, she knew that she couldn't take much more of their searing current.

"Flash!" she shouted. "Search the buildings! Find the controls for the facility's power and shut it down! Hurry!"

Flash quickly finished bringing the last two employees to safety. "You got it, Princess!" he yelled back. "'Hurry' is my middle name. Actually, Rudolph is my middle name, but 'Hurry' is so much cooler."

Dashing from building to building, the Flash scanned each room, each wall, searching for the controls to shut down the complex's main power, as chunks of debris crumbled all around him. Reaching the last building, he found the main power controls.

Flash grabbed the massive switch—two long metal prongs attached by a thick wooden handle—thinking, *Didn't I see a switch like this in a Frankenstein movie once?* Then he yanked on the rusty old control, removing it from two tiny pincers at the top, then connecting it to a set of identical pincers below.

As he tore from the building, it collapsed behind him in a smoky heap.

Back at the reactor's base, the snaking cables dropped lifelessly to the ground. Wonder Woman released her grip on the lasso, then toppled over from exhaustion and the effects of the electric shocks. Flash streaked up beside her as she collapsed, catching her just before she hit the ground.

"Are you okay, Diana?" he asked, placing her down gently.

"Yes, thank you," she replied, slowly getting to her feet, rubbing her eyes.

"It looks like the aftershocks have stopped," reported Hawkgirl as she landed beside them. The powerful winged warrior appeared to be as energetic and ready for action as she had been before vaporizing all the building fragments with her mace. Sparks flew from her weapon, however, which was damaged from the repetitive smashing of concrete and bricks.

"Yes," Wonder Woman agreed. "The situation here appears to be stable. But I wonder how Superman and Green Lantern are making out."

The blue atmosphere of Earth vanished quickly, giving way to the endless blackness of space, as Superman and Green Lantern flew the overheating nuclear reactor away from the planet's surface. Green Lantern's force field allowed Superman to breathe in space.

"Let's get this thing safely out of the solar system," Superman said as they flew past Mars.

"I don't know how much longer the reactor's going to last," Green Lantern pointed out. "We may not have a—"

KA-FOOOM!

The radioactive core of the reactor finally reached its critical mass. Exploding like an atomic bomb, the tall circular tower shattered in Superman's hands. The Man of Steel tensed all his muscles and took a deep breath as Green Lantern instinctively removed Superman from his force field.

As the Man of Steel held his breath, Green Lantern maintained his force field around the explosion, containing the blast and preventing the deadly radiation from washing over Superman and then spreading out into space. Using the full power of his ring, the Emerald Warrior absorbed the nuclear energy into his own powerful green light, drawing it back into the ring. He then extended his force field over Superman again so that the Man of Steel could breathe during the trip back to Earth.

Shaking his head to ease the ringing in his ears, Superman clasped Green Lantern firmly on the shoulder. "Nice work," he said to his friend, nodding.

"I was just about to say the same thing to you," Green Lantern replied.

When the two heroes returned to their teammates back on Earth, they were joined by the administrator of the nuclear facility, plus a group of Russian political and military leaders.

"We wish to express our deep gratitude to these heroes from the West," the administrator announced to the crowd. "You have now truly become great heroes here in Russia as well!"

CHAPTER 5

Not far from the smoldering remains of the Pavlovich Nuclear Energy Facility, in an underground laboratory deep beneath the Ural Mountains, electrical power that had flowed steadily to the long-forgotten lab suddenly shut off.

The underground power line led from a large vault-like chamber within the lab out through the mountain, emerging at the now-destroyed nuclear facility. For over twenty years, the small branching electrical cable split off from the reactor's main power line. It supplied the nearby laboratory's cryogenic freezing chamber with the power needed to maintain five individuals in perfect states of hibernation.

When Flash threw the main power switch, cutting

off electricity at the doomed nuclear facility, he had unknowingly shut down the power supply to the freezing chamber in the hidden lab.

Slowly, the cryogenic chamber thawed out, its temperature rising half a degree each hour. When the temperature inside the chamber finally drifted above the freezing mark, the bodies within began to stir.

One by one the five figures flexed their fingers, then wrists, elbows, knees, and ankles, stretching stiff limbs, as vague memories drifted to the surface of their consciousness. The thawing process ended, and the massive steel door to the chamber swung open.

Although the power to the chamber was off, the rest of the lab was supplied by a separate generator, hidden within the lab itself. Harsh fluorescent light flooded the vault, causing those within to squint until their long-dormant eyes adjusted to the brightness.

A tall, barrel-chested man led the others from the chamber. His large bulging muscles rippled along the length of his body. His red hair was close-cropped and his copper-colored beard spread evenly across his finely chiseled face. A green uniform—vaguely military in design—with red stripes running along the sides covered his massive frame. A bright red cape hung from his shoulders.

"So," the man spoke, his voice rough and raspy from decades of disuse. "Red Dawn has been revived."

The woman beside him spoke next. She was slender and moved with grace and quickness, despite the years of hibernation. Her flaming red hair reached down to her narrow shoulders, and her olive green costume fit tightly against her skin.

"Look around, Red Fury," she said, pointing to the empty control room. "You are our leader. You know that we were to be awakened by our military commanders in the event of a national emergency or a war with the West. But who has awakened us? We are alone in this laboratory."

"Blaze is correct," said the third member of the group, a tall, thin being, half man, half bird. Huge gray wings extended from his bony back, and a thin ridge ran along the center of his skull. His long legs and broad chest were covered in a tight black and purple uniform. A sharp beak protruded from his slender face, and his birdlike feet had three claws in the front and one more sticking out from his heel. "This is most odd. I had expected to find a roomful of generals awaiting our revival."

A squat, powerful woman of solid muscle walked slowly up beside Red Fury. She looked like a champion weight lifter. Her uniform resembled that of the group's leader, a green top trimmed in red. But unlike Red Fury's more formal costume, her shirt dipped down around the neck, and the short sleeves revealed her muscular arms. Brown leather cuffs surrounded her wrists, matching the color of her boots and the thick belt that wrapped around her waist. It looked like a belt that would be worn by a heavyweight boxing champion.

"We are wasting time, Gray Heron," the woman said harshly to the winged member of Red Dawn. "We should not be discussing generals, we should be finding out what situation has caused our awakening! What do you say, Beacon?"

"I agree with you, Sinew," replied the final member of the group, a trim man in a tight-fitting yellow bodysuit. Beneath his shock of jet-black hair, a yellow band with a large glittering gemstone in its center surrounded his forehead. The gem glowed with a radiant yellow aura. "Let us assess our current situation, then move into action."

Not waiting for a response, Beacon fired a broad yellow beam from his gemstone. The swath of shimmering light flooded the control room, activating the long-silent computer system. Although this room had not lost power when the line at the reactor had been switched off, Beacon's energy beam jump-started the dormant equipment that now sprung to life as if it had been used mere hours—rather than decades—ago.

Red Fury sat at the control panel of the lab's main computer and activated its communications system. "I will contact Soviet High Command," he announced. "Surely they will be able to fill us in on the current situation."

Red Dawn's leader sent out a signal using the secret frequency established for the Soviet High Command, the Soviet Union's top military body. After a few seconds, only hiss and static returned through the small speaker on the control panel.

"Nothing!" Red Fury exclaimed.

"Apparently, the frequency is no longer in use," Beacon concluded.

"Why don't we investigate the situation firsthand," Blaze suggested, anxious to be outside and moving quickly. Speed was at the core of her nature, and standing around—not to mention spending several decades in hibernation—always got her antsy. "Let's go see what world we have awakened to!"

Red Fury nodded in agreement, then led the others from the lab.

The chilly night air felt refreshing as it rushed past Blaze's face. After many years of breathing recycled, artificially refrigerated air, the natural breezes smelled sweet, like a gentle waft of fine perfume. As she raced through the misty darkness, Blaze realized just how long it had been since she'd actually run. For the first time since reawakening she felt truly alive, like someone starved for oxygen finally taking a deep breath.

The countryside all around her melted into a blur as she picked up speed. This was what she was meant to do, what she was created for—running—fast, endless running. The thrill of motion coursed through her veins, Red Dawn's predicament forgotten for the moment.

In the sky above Blaze, her teammates flew through the night, matching her pace when they could. Every so often she would put on a burst of speed, out of sheer excitement, and lose the others. Then she would adjust her velocity, and her teammates would catch up.

Red Fury soared, his arms extended before him, his dark red cape rippling as he moved. Sinew—the other member of Red Dawn incapable of flight—held on to him tightly, her thick muscular arms wrapped around his chest.

Gray Heron gracefully flapped his huge wings, flying above the others. Riding wind currents, he seemed to relish the freedom of flight, appearing completely at home in the sky.

Beacon brought up the rear. A shimmering yellow aura extended from the gem on his forehead, surrounding his body. Its energy propelled him forward.

In a short while, as Red Dawn neared the remains of the Pavlovich Nuclear Energy Facility, Blaze let out a gasp. Slowing to a stop as her teammates landed beside her, the fastest member of the group surveyed the damage at the now-deserted site.

Smoke and steam still poured steadily from the base upon which the mighty nuclear reactor had stood. The crumbled ruins of buildings lay strewn everywhere. The devastation was almost incomprehensible.

"It appears as if this power plant has been attacked," Blaze surmised.

"Perhaps that is why we have been awakened," suggested Sinew as she sifted through still-smoldering rubble.

"We must continue our exploration," ordered Red Fury, "in Moscow, Mother Russia's greatest city."

With the other members of Red Dawn once again in the sky above her, Blaze tore through towns and open wilderness, until the skyline of Moscow grew steadily larger in her view. Wishing to remain unseen in the bustling city, with her teammates flying high above, Blaze kept her speed up as she raced from street to street, stunned by what she saw.

What has happened here? she thought, certain that the others were equally disturbed by the shocking changes to the great Russian city. Moving too swiftly to be seen, Blaze entered an American-style fast-food restaurant. As she zoomed around the dining area, Blaze watched in horror as Russian teenagers wolfed down greasy burgers, giant orders of fries, and big buckets of fried chicken.

Remaining unseen, Blaze overheard several conversations.

"Did you double-size those fries, dude?" one pimply-faced teenaged girl asked the boy who had just joined her at the table, carrying a tray packed with food.

"Well, duh," the boy replied. "I got what you wanted: two mega burgers with extra cheese, a double-sized order of mega fries, and two mega shakes."

"Awesome!" the girl cried, taking a huge bite from her burger, ketchup dripping down her chin.

American fast food in Moscow? Blaze wondered as

she sped out of the restaurant. *How can this be?* Then she dashed off to continue exploring the city.

In an alley not far from Blaze, Red Fury landed, placing Sinew down beside him. "We must split up to cover more ground," Red Fury announced. "Find out what you can, but remain unseen. We'll meet in one hour at the rendezvous point just outside the city."

Sinew nodded, then moved stealthily away.

Red Fury hugged the shadows, flying quickly and quietly above the streets. His rage grew as he passed one upscale store after another. Each display window screamed out at him in strange, disturbing words:

BIG STEREO SALE! 40% OFF!

WE'VE GOT THE SHOES THAT
KEEP YOU ON THE MOVE!

IF YOU'RE NOT WEARING OUR PANTS,
YOU MIGHT AS WELL NOT BE WEARING
ANY PANTS AT ALL!!

A crowd of young people moved swiftly down the street toward Red Fury, carrying shopping bags filled with recent purchases, laughing and joking. In a moment they would spot him, and he was in no mood to explain his presence, much less his costume.

The leader of Red Dawn ducked into the nearest doorway and found himself inside the Café Americana, a three-story restaurant packed with diners. Red Fury leapt straight up, flying close to the wall, speeding to the restaurant's highest level, which appeared to be deserted.

Peering down at the loud, frantic scene below, Red Fury used his enhanced hearing ability to listen in on conversations among the patrons.

"I'd like the New York salad, with extra dressing, please," one man said as his waiter jotted down the order.

"I'll take the California club sandwich, please," a woman ordered.

"I want the Washington potato puffs!" a young girl screamed.

"Politely, Jennifer," her mother chided. "Now, tell the man what you want, but remember to say 'please.'"

As Red Fury took in the various conversations, a voice from behind startled him.

"Hey, man, what are you dressed up for?" asked a teenager as he stepped from the men's room, giggling at Red Fury's costume and cape. "What are you, celebrating Halloween?"

Red Fury vanished in a streaking blur, flying from the restaurant, his mind reeling.

Sinew marched down a busy street, trying her best to remain unseen, but failing miserably. She did not have Blaze's speed or Red Fury's flying ability, and so as she moved along the sidewalk, passersby stared for a moment, then chalked up her appearance to that of a weight lifter or a circus performer.

On a crowded corner, Sinew stepped into a coffee bar. Groups of young people sipped hot beverages of all varieties, chatting or working at notebook computers.

"Have you tried the triple chocolate latte with a shot of espresso?" one young woman asked her friend. "It's, like, heavenly!"

A long line of people extended from the service window. "I'll have a half-caf, half-decaf vanilla mocha hazelnut frappe with a scoop of cappuccino ice cream, please," a young man ordered.

"Two iced chai lattes and a fat-free oat bran muffin," another man requested of the uniform-clad server at the window.

It was all Sinew could do to restrain herself from tearing the place apart. *Capitalism run rampant!* she thought as she stormed from the coffee bar back out onto the street.

Gray Heron folded his wings and gently landed on the roof of a large clothing store. As he had approached the store, he had noticed a sign in the front window that read SPECIAL TODAY: RELAXED FIT JEANS! and he was baffled as to its possible meaning. Leaning over the roof's edge, he peered down at the customers passing in and out of the front door, their conversations drifting up to his high perch.

"They were all out of the extra-extra-large jeans," a thin teenaged boy complained. "I hope the extra-large ones I got don't look stupid on me."

"I already have that fleece pullover in red, black, and green," a teenaged girl explained to her friend. "But I just had to have it in beige!"

Out of control consumerism, Gray Heron thought. *How did this happen here?* Stretching his wings to their full impressive span, he lifted himself back into the sky.

Beacon landed across the street from a giant appliance store. Staring at the window filled with television sets, he was stunned and confused by the images flashing on the screens.

One set showed a group of young men and women in their twenties gathered in a large apartment. Some appeared to be arguing, others laughing, still others kissing. As the show ended, everyone in the apartment joined in a huge group hug.

Another TV showed a courtroom with a lawyer making an impassioned plea to a jury. What looked like a group of castaways made their way around a tropical island on another screen, some arguing, others whispering conspiratorially.

The last screen showed a woman in a tall chair with bright spotlights sweeping and flashing all around her, and a man in a suit apparently asking questions. Each time she gave a correct answer, the crowd watching her applauded and she sighed with relief.

Shaking his head, Beacon surrounded himself with his power beam and took once again to the air.

By the time the others all joined Blaze on the outskirts of the city, she had formed a few conclusions of her own. As Red Dawn finished gathering, the green-clad speedster spoke first.

"American food, American clothes, American everything!" she began. "It's difficult to know what country we are in!"

"American television shows on every set I saw," Beacon reported.

"A store devoted to selling nothing but . . . but coffee!" Sinew said, spitting out the words with contempt.

"Capitalism run wild in Moscow?" Gray Heron asked the question on everyone's mind. "How can this have happened?"

Red Fury sighed. "It is simple," he said firmly. "They attacked our power plant, and they have taken over our greatest city. Obviously while we were in hibernation, the United States invaded Russia, and because for some reason we were not awakened, the United States won!"

Red Dawn sped back to their lab to see if they could gather more details on the apparent American takeover of Russia. Red Fury sat before the lab's main computer, searching until he found the correct frequency for a functioning Russian intelligence system. Tied into an orbiting satellite, the system beamed television images and newspaper archives to the computer's large monitor. The others gathered behind him, looking over his broad shoulders.

"It appears that we have awakened early in the twenty-first century," Red Fury reported. Then the five members of Red Dawn watched in stunned amazement as they reviewed the astonishing events of the past twenty-plus years.

Through television news reports and newspaper articles, they learned of the end of the Cold War. The Soviet Union's tense competition with the United States and the other Western world powers had been the dominant factor in both nations at the time of Red Dawn's creation. They had been trained to distrust the West. In fact, it was their entire reason for being.

Images of the Berlin Wall coming down stunned the group. It had been one of the most visible symbols of the East/West divide. Learning of the breakup of the Soviet Union into individual countries shocked them as well. Finally, stories of the growth of capitalism and the end of the communist system in Russia were almost more than they could handle.

"According to all this, there was no war," Red Fury said as the images of a changed world continued flashing before him.

"The Americans are obviously controlling the media,"

said Blaze, "as we did for so many years. They want the world to believe that this change was agreed to by both countries, and that we are all friends now." Blaze's quick and agile mind leapt to the only possible conclusion based on her horrifying visit to Moscow.

"Then their victory is complete," Sinew added, rage coloring her voice.

"Red Fury, I think we should learn what we can of General Kolnikov and Dr. Pushkin," Blaze suggested. "Our answers may be found with them."

Red Fury agreed, unable, along with the rest of Red Dawn, to find a way to reconcile these great changes. Searching for information now about the two men responsible for project Red Dawn, Red Fury discovered several astounding newspaper reports.

"Here," he said, pointing to an article on the screen. "According to this, Dr. Pushkin was killed in a car accident, not long after we were placed in the cryogenic chamber."

"And what of the general?" Sinew asked.

An exhaustive search turned up no indication of General Kolnikov's whereabouts. Red Fury found a few small references to the general in articles all dating from the mid- to late 1970s. But after that, nothing, as if he had vanished from the face of the Earth.

Blaze shook her head impatiently. "So we still don't know why we were not awakened during the war, or how and why we were taken out of hibernation now," she said, frustrated by their limited success in finding answers. "Clearly, General Kolnikov and Dr. Pushkin had nothing to do with it."

"Wait!" Sinew exclaimed suddenly. "Look!" Pointing at the monitor, she and the others intently watched a report of the recent accident at the Pavlovich Nuclear Energy Facility.

Images of the five heroes of the Justice League in action filled the screen: Hawkgirl streaking through the air, smashing concrete chunks with her mace; Wonder Woman using her Golden Lasso to help secure the crumbling reactor; Green Lantern using the energy from his power ring first as a narrow cutting beam, then as a broad shield; Superman tearing the reactor from its base and flying off into space with it; and the Flash racing at top speed, hustling people to safety, then turning off the power.

"Perhaps the loss of power there had some effect on the cryogenic chamber," Beacon suggested as scenes of the Justice League's rescue efforts continued.

Red Dawn sat silently for a few more seconds, transfixed by the stunning display unfolding on the monitor.

"We were right!" Red Fury shouted. "Americans operating in Russia! They must have made their attack look like an accident so that they could come to the rescue!"

"Yes," Blaze said, still staring at the screen. "And it appears that they have banded together into this Justice League, as they call it."

The news report wrapped up with an image of the administrator of the nuclear facility standing beside a group of Russian political and military leaders.

"We wish to express our deep gratitude to these heroes from the West," said the administrator. "You have now truly become great heroes here in Russia, as well!"

Red Fury seethed. Standing suddenly, his chair flying into the wall behind him, he drew back his massive fist and punched a hole through the monitor. Glass fragments sprayed around the control room, and sparks and smoke drifted up from the shattered screen. Pieces of the damaged system dangled uselessly from the control panel.

"Heroes of Russia!" he bellowed, pacing from one end of the control room to the other. "Bah! *We* were to be the heroes of Russia. And now, we must destroy the Justice League and take back our rightful roles."

Red Fury stared at the smashed monitor before him. "Beacon," he shouted. "Can you fix this?"

"I can take another monitor and run it into the system," Beacon—the most technically skilled of the group—explained. Within a few minutes, the new monitor was up and running. Beacon sat at the control panel as Red Fury continued to pace.

"Access historical records of the United States," Red Fury ordered. "Specifically, information about famous sites and monuments."

"I'm afraid you destroyed more than just the monitor," Beacon informed Red Fury. "It appears that some of the system's memory was also damaged. Some files appear to be irretrievable. I'll do my best, though."

Hours later, Beacon finally managed to find what Red Fury was searching for. One by one, photos of the United States scrolled along the monitor. Pausing at one particular photograph, Red Fury smiled for the first time since his revival from hibernation.

"That's it!" he cried, calling the others to his side, then pointing at the monitor. "This is where we will confront the mighty heroes of the West. It will be a fitting locale for their defeat!"

CHAPTER 6

On board the Watchtower, Flash paced nervously from one room to the next. His version of pacing consisted of zooming up to each of his teammates, peering over his or her shoulder, and asking lots of questions.

Following the Justice League's heroics at the nuclear reactor, Flash was hesitant to return home and resume his life as Wally West. He had missed a job interview while helping to rescue people at the disaster in Russia, and the thought of continuing his endless search for employment made him nauseous.

The truth was, he felt more comfortable racing around in his bright red costume, his face half covered by a mask, than he did when he was Wally West.

As a hero, he had earned the respect of his team-mates and the gratitude of millions.

Flash raced around the main observation deck of the Watchtower, stopping behind Superman and J'onn J'onzz. The two heroes were hard at work, analyzing readings from the Watchtower's deep space telescope.

"Find any new planets or nebulas or cool cosmic dust?" Flash asked, slurping an iced mocha from the Watchtower's fully stocked kitchen. He glanced down at the stream of numbers scrolling quickly up a monitor.

Superman looked right at him. "We're a little busy here," he said, raising his eyebrows.

"Perhaps you should practice on your own the relaxation techniques I have shown you," J'onn suggested.

"Oh, I don't think I'm ready to solo yet, J'onn," Flash replied. "But I get the message. I'll go see what the others are up to."

Before J'onn could reply, Flash vanished. Without giving him another thought, the Martian Manhunter and the Man of Steel turned back to their work.

Flash sped up the circular staircase leading from the observation deck to one of the small laboratories on the upper floor of the Watchtower. There he found Green Lantern helping Hawkgirl repair her damaged mace. The sophisticated, high-tech weapon lay open on a metal lab table. Green Lantern carefully repaired tiny nanocircuits with a finely concentrated beam from his power ring as Hawkgirl rotated the mace.

"Anybody thirsty?" Flash asked, extending a cup of iced mocha toward his teammates. Condensation from the outside of the cup dripped onto the open circuits of the weapon, sending a plume of acrid white smoke up into Green Lantern's face.

"What did I tell you about drinks in the lab?" Green Lantern shouted at Flash, coughing from the burning smoke in his throat. "You just cost us two hours' work!'"

"Oops," Flash said, grinning sheepishly. "Looks like I'm in the way here, too. I'll just—"

beepbeepbeepbeep

They were suddenly interrupted by a tiny alarm that sounded on the control panel in the lab. Switching off his power ring, Green Lantern stepped up to the panel and punched a button. The image of Wonder Woman appeared on a small monitor.

"What's going on?" Green Lantern asked.

"We just got a report from General Welles of strange activity at the Mount Rushmore monument," Wonder Woman explained over the communications system.

"What kind of 'strange activity'?" Green Lantern asked as the others in the room gathered around him.

"Five costumed individuals, apparently with superpowers, have taken up positions among the giant faces of the presidents on the mountainside," Diana explained. "One is flying around carrying another, one has body-length wings, one is glowing yellow, and one is moving so fast that the military people can't make out what he—or maybe she—even looks like. And someone has carved into the mountainside, 'Bring us the Justice League!'

"It could just be a hoax of some kind, but the general asked us to check it out. I'll go do some advance scouting and let you know if it's necessary for the rest of you to join me."

"Why don't you take the Flash with you, Diana," Green Lantern suggested, seeing a chance to get the Scarlet Speedster out of his hair.

"I can take a hint," Flash said, actually thrilled by the idea of going on a mission with Wonder Woman. "Okay with you, Princess?"

"Fine," Wonder Woman replied.

"Cool," said the Flash. "A chance to go fight some bad guys!"

"If they *are* bad guys," Green Lantern replied, trying to focus on the delicate repair work before him. "They could just be some weirdos in costumes."

"Flying and glowing weirdos in costumes?" Flash asked.

"Take one of Batman's DNA scanners with you," Green Lantern suggested, ignoring the question. "See if you can get a reading on these people so we can search for matches. We may have dealt with them before."

"Will do," Flash said. "Diana, I'll meet you at the launching bay."

Wonder Woman and Flash boarded the *Javelin-7* and streaked toward Earth. Landing a short distance away from the Mount Rushmore national monument in South Dakota, they hurried to the huge granite outcropping. Peering down from the top of the sixty-foot-tall sculpted busts of four U.S. presidents, the heroes spotted the five costumed figures.

Red Fury stood atop George Washington's nose, hands on hips, his red cape fluttering in the wind. Gray Heron crouched on top of Thomas Jefferson's head. His body-length wings were spread wide open, as if he were about to take flight. Perched on Theodore Roosevelt's thick moustache, Beacon's yellow gemstone glowed brightly.

The remaining two members of Red Dawn, Sinew and Blaze, each stood upon Abraham Lincoln's bushy eyebrows.

The Flash looked across the open gorge to the sheer cliff face on the other side. There, carved into the mountain, were the words BRING US THE JUSTICE LEAGUE!

Who are these freaks? Flash wondered, staring down in disbelief. *And how did they get out onto the monument?*

"Where are the other members of the Justice League?" Red Fury shouted. "We demanded the entire team."

"Demanded?" Wonder Woman shouted back. "Who are you, and what do you want with us?"

Red Fury leapt from the long, carved face, flying

slowly up to where the heroes stood. He hovered in midair, face to face with the Amazon Princess.

"What do we want?" he repeated, his cold green eyes locked on hers. "Justice. We want justice for the people of the Soviet Union. They do not need heroes from the West. For we are Red Dawn, and we have awakened to claim our rightful place in the world!"

"The Soviet Union?" Flash blurted out, barely able to stifle a giggle. "Maybe you missed the paper, buddy, but the Soviet Union hasn't existed for more than a decade. What rock have you been buried under?"

"Lies!" shouted Sinew. She leapt from the bust of Lincoln, climbing up the side of the mountain toward the heroes. Her powerful fingers dug into the granite for support. "We will show the world true heroes and avenge your destruction of our power plant!"

"Destruction!" Wonder Woman countered in disbelief. "Apparently you have been receiving false information. We saved the Russian people from a major disaster!"

"Only to gain favor in the ongoing battle with the West!" Sinew cried. Reaching the top of the mountain, she pointed an accusing finger. "When we have shown the world that Red Dawn is stronger, we will be celebrated as Soviet heroes."

"The Cold War is over, beautiful," Flash replied quickly, winking at the squat muscular powerhouse. As he spoke, his hand moved to a small device hidden in his belt. Swiftly and silently he took a DNA scan of Sinew. "We're all friends now. You know, friends? Maybe we can help get you a job with the National Wrestling League. They're always looking for colorful new characters, and you, sweetheart, most definitely fit the bill."

"Enough talk!" Sinew cried. Enraged by Flash's seemingly endless babble, she charged at the Scarlet Speedster like a crazed bull.

Flash easily sidestepped Sinew, then he glanced down and spotted Blaze.

"Whoa!" he cried. "Maybe I can talk some sense into your friend there." Streaking along the side of Lincoln's face, Flash stopped suddenly beside Blaze.

She had been watching the confrontation, listening to Flash's words, not the least bit surprised he would claim that the Cold War was over and the U.S. and Russia were now friends. Blaze stared at Flash, admittedly amazed and intrigued by his display of speed.

"You realize that your pal there is a couple of rubles shy of the full fare, if you know what I mean," Flash quipped, pointing up toward Sinew. "You, on the other hand. Wow! Whaddaya say we take a spin around the world two or three times! By the way, what's your name?"

Before Blaze could respond, Flash took off in a crimson blur, hoping she would follow. Her curiosity piqued, she raced after him, quickly catching up. "I am called Blaze," she said. "And you?"

Mimicking Flash's move, Blaze increased her speed, pulling away before he could reply.

Oh, I like her! Flash thought. *She's fast. I mean,* really *fast! Could she possibly be faster than me? Nah!* Pushing himself harder, Flash caught up to Blaze.

"Nice moves," he said. "They remind me of someone . . . me! Flash is the name, and nobody's faster. Nobody."

"You speak with great confidence, Flash," Blaze responded. "But I speak for the Russian people, who need true heroes. Perhaps *I* should be the one wearing the *red* costume, not you! It might be more appropriate, don't you think?"

"Clever," Flash said, impressed by her wit. "Funny. I see it's not only your feet that are quick. So, come on, what do you guys really want?"

"To defeat you," Blaze replied, smiling. Then she veered sharply, vanishing from view.

Flash slowed to a stop. He had finally met a woman who could keep up with him. The last thing he wanted was a fight. Unfortunately, Red Dawn had other ideas.

ZZAATT!

Beacon fired a yellow energy blast from his gemstone, striking Flash in the back. The force of the jolt sent the Scarlet Speedster tumbling over the side of the mountaintop, plunging toward the rocky gorge far below.

Wonder Woman leapt from the top of the monument, soaring through the air, picking up speed as she flew toward the plummeting crimson-clad hero. Landing in the gorge just seconds before Flash would have hit the ground, the Amazon Princess caught him in her arms, then placed him on his feet.

"Nice catch, Princess," Flash said. "Thanks. Looks like our playmates mean business."

"Perhaps we should call the others," Wonder Woman suggested, scanning the sky for another attack.

"Nah," Flash replied. "We can handle this, and I don't want to escalate the situation if we don't have to. That would only convince them more that we're the bad guys."

Wonder Woman nodded her agreement, just as Gray Heron swooped toward her, his great wings spread wide.

"I'll handle him," she said to Flash. "You check on the others."

"Gotcha," Flash replied, happy to oblige if it meant catching up to Blaze. He tore away, racing back up the sheer lower section of the mountain, then scrambling up and over the carved face of Teddy Roosevelt, in search of the female speedster.

Wonder Woman unfurled her Golden Lasso. Timing her throw perfectly, she tossed the gleaming rope skyward. It looped around Gray Heron's wings, pinning them to his side. Yanking hard on the lasso, she cinched it securely. Unable to use his wings, Gray Heron crashed to the ground, dazed from the impact.

Now I can learn the truth about Red Dawn, Diana thought, landing beside Gray Heron. Her Golden Lasso had the amazing ability to force the person caught in it to speak only the truth. However, the truth would have to wait.

Wonder Woman looked up and spotted Red Fury and Beacon flying toward her. Quickly pulling her Golden Lasso from Gray Heron, she sent it curling back toward herself. Snatching the rope from the air, she secured it to her belt.

Beacon's body was surrounded by a yellow energy field radiating from the gemstone on his forehead. The Amazon Princess braced for a blast from Beacon, like the one that had struck the Flash, but none came.

He must be unable to fire those blasts while using his gemstone's power to fly, she thought. At that moment, Red Fury—speeding through the sky with his thickly gloved fists extended before him—fired twin beams of glowing red energy from his eyes.

Great Hera! Wonder Woman thought. *Not only does he possess the power of flight, but he can fire heat energy from his eyes as well!* She lifted her arms and deflected the searing beams with her two silver bracelets. The scarlet streaks reflected off the metal wrist cuffs, shot back into the air, and struck Beacon in the midsection. Instantly, his yellow power aura vanished, and he tumbled to the ground, landing in a heap.

That left only Red Fury, who still streaked toward her. *What other powers might he possess?* Diana wondered as she prepared herself for combat. *Still, as Red Dawn's leader, he would have the answers I seek.*

As Wonder Woman reached for her lasso, Red Fury

slammed into her with tremendous power. Having braced for the impact, though, the Amazon Warrior shifted her weight to the side, shoving Red Fury as he rushed past her. But the leader of Red Dawn was fast and clever. He reached out and grabbed her waist, sending the two combatants tumbling to the rocky ground.

As Flash reached the top of the mountain, Sinew stepped right in his path.

BOOF!

The Scarlet Speedster bounced off her powerful compact body and went sprawling to the ground. It felt as if he had slammed into a brick wall.

"Your partner down in the gorge will fail," Sinew boasted. "Just as you will fail here!"

"Yeah, right, whatever," Flash muttered, scrambling to his feet. "Don't they get the History Channel in your part of the world, lady? The Cold War is over!"

What am I wasting time with this pit bull for? Flash wondered. *I've got to find Blaze.* "Well, it's been lovely chatting with you," Flash quipped. He raced toward Sinew, then ran in a blinding circle around her, going faster and faster, talking almost as quickly as he moved. "Let's do it again, say in two or three decades. Maybe by then you'll have joined the twenty-first century. It's really awesome. We have satellite dishes, cell phones, the Internet, commercials at the movies. All right, so maybe it's not perfect."

WHOOSH!

The air surrounding Sinew spun into a tornado-like vortex, lifting and disposing of her several hundred yards away. Flash then slowed to a stop.

"You think you're pretty cool, don't you?" said a voice from behind him.

Whirling around, Flash found himself face to face with Blaze.

"Where have you been?" he asked.

"Speeding around the area, checking to see if any more of your friends were around," she explained, taking off in an emerald-tinged streak.

"I hate it when she does that," Flash said, zooming after Blaze. "I've had women run out on me, but this is ridiculous."

The two speedsters tore across the mountaintop, one taking the lead, then the other.

"Why aren't you down there in the gorge helping your buddies?" Flash asked as the gray granite all around them smeared into a streaky blur.

"I could ask you the same question," Blaze replied without missing a beat.

"Let me answer for you," he shot back.

"Do I have a choice?" she asked.

"You're not down there helping because you know I'm right," Flash said. "I don't know why the big guy in the cape and that human bowling ball I just ran into are telling you that we're still enemies, but I believe you know that we're not. Don't you think that if we were committed to your destruction, we would have brought the entire Justice League to wipe you out, to show what great 'heroes' we were, rather than just sending our little two-person scouting team?"

KA-THOOM!

Before Blaze could respond, both she and Flash slowed down at the sound of an explosion, followed by a deep rumbling in the gorge below.

"Uh-oh," Flash said, coming to a halt. "That's not a good sound. Not good at all."

Down in the gorge, Wonder Woman and Red Fury grasped each other's shoulders, struggling in a contest of pure power.

"You are strong," he admitted. "For a woman."

"For a—?" Wonder Woman couldn't even bring herself to repeat the phrase. "I am a born warrior, and I fear no man!"

"Not even one who can scorch you with a mere glance?" Red Fury replied, focusing his eyes squarely on Wonder Woman's head. As he tightened his grasp on the Amazon Warrior's arms, preventing her from deflecting the blast again, Red Fury attempted to fire beams of heat from his eyes.

Nothing happened.

The leader of Red Dawn suddenly felt dizzy and weak. His face turned bright red, sweat broke out on his forehead, and his powerful hands began to tremble. *What is happening to me?* Red Fury thought as he felt his strength desert him. *I have never felt so tired, so helpless.*

In Red Fury's weakened state, Wonder Woman's power became more than he could handle. With a mighty shove, she forced him to the ground, then surrounded him with her Lasso of Truth.

"Now, you will tell me what all this is about!" she demanded as her weakened opponent struggled to catch his breath.

"Red Dawn in hibernation," Red Fury gasped, struggling to stay conscious, yet firmly under the lasso's truth-inducing power. "Justice League attacked power plant. America invaded Russia. American stores, music, food, everything. We are defeated, but Red Dawn will take control and make Russia great again. We will be the heroes. News reports of U.S.-Soviet friendship a lie. All American propaganda."

Panic swept over Red Fury as he spoke, unable to stop the words from pouring out, and feeling the very life force draining from his body. Standing, he stumbled away from Wonder Woman, falling back to the ground, unconscious, landing beside Beacon and Gray Heron.

As Wonder Woman pulled her lasso from Red Fury, Beacon awoke, took in this unexpected turn of events, then focused all his energy at a ledge high on the sheer face of the mountain across from the famous sculptures, and directly above the Amazon Warrior.

ZZAATT! KA-RAK!

The ledge shattered and tumbled down the mountain in a raging rockslide.

Before she realized what had happened, Diana felt herself being scooped into the arms of an unseen rescuer.

THOOM!

The massive pile of rocks struck the ground at the base of the mountain, right where Wonder Woman had been standing. A deafening rumble and billowing plumes of dust radiated from the rocks, blanketing the gorge.

Safely clear of the rockslide, Flash slowed to a gradual stop, then placed Wonder Woman on her feet.

"My turn to say thanks," she said as the two heroes squinted through the dust, looking for movement in the rubble. When the thick gray clouds finally settled, they could see no sign of Red Dawn.

"They're gone!" Flash exclaimed. "All of them."

"I believe they were all clear of the rockslide," Diana explained. "It appears that they have simply vanished!"

CHAPTER
7

The *Javelin-7* eased into its docking bay on the Watchtower. Inside the shuttle, Flash and Wonder Woman were still trying to make sense of the five beings with whom they had just done battle.

"How could a team of super heroes be running around in Russia without any of us knowing about them?" Flash asked as the final docking clamps snapped into place. "Certainly Supes or Bats would have been aware of anyone with powers like that. Or J'onn would have sensed them telepathically. They did say something about awakening, though."

"Yes," Wonder Woman replied. "I managed to get some information from Red Fury before he passed out. He mentioned being in hibernation. He also believes that the United States invaded Russia, and that all news reports about recent events are lies. 'American propaganda,' he called it."

"Well, that's a switch," Flash commented as the docking sequence ended. "Time was, we believed everything the Russians said to be propaganda."

The two emerged from the ship and headed right for the main observation deck, where Green Lantern was waiting for them. Flash and Wonder Woman quickly filled the Emerald Warrior in on what they had learned.

"Where are the others?" Wonder Woman asked.

"The report of your battle has been all over the news. Apparently Red Dawn's activity at Mount Rushmore has caused an international incident," Green Lantern explained. "The World Assembly called an emergency session. The U.S. ambassador wants to know what five superpowered Russians are doing defacing one of their national monuments, and the Russians have gotten their backs up calling the accusation an insult worthy of the old Cold War days. Superman, J'onn, and Hawkgirl have gone to Metropolis as representatives of the Justice League to address the assembly and try to help sort this out. They're waiting for a more detailed report from

us so that they can tell the diplomats what's going
on.

"Meanwhile, Batman has been following these
events, and he's been doing some research into the
names. I've got him on video comm link."

The three heroes gathered around the Watchtower's
main computer as the image of Batman appeared on a
small monitor. He was in the Batcave, using the
Batcomputer to assist the team.

"I searched through some old KGB files that have
recently been declassified," Batman explained. "I was
able to locate a reference to 'Red Dawn.'"

"Any mention of a speedy redhead?" Flash asked
excitedly. He understood the importance of discover-
ing the truth behind the bizarre arrival of this group
of superpowered individuals, but he simply could not
get Blaze off his mind.

"Later, hotshot," Green Lantern reprimanded him.
"Let the man talk."

Batman continued. "Red Dawn was a secret Soviet
project put together in the late 1970s," he reported.
"They are a group of genetically engineered metahumans. Red Dawn was a kind of fail-safe defense, a
last resort if the Cold War ever heated up. These five

were placed into cryogenic freeze in a hidden location somewhere in the Ural Mountains. They were to be revived only in the event of a war with the West."

"The Urals!" Green Lantern exclaimed. "But that's where the earthquake and the nuclear reactor were. Could we have done something to pull these Cold War relics out of their deep freeze?"

"It's possible," Batman replied. "My research shows that project Red Dawn was headed by a General Kolnikov. But according to the KBG, Kolnikov vanished mysteriously shortly after Red Dawn was placed into cryogenic freeze. Also, the lead scientist on the project died in a car crash right around the same time.

"Seems to me that our first priority would be to locate the general, if he's still alive. He might be able to convince these metahumans that their original mission is now obsolete."

"Agreed," Green Lantern replied. "But where do we start?"

"Flash, did you get DNA scans of the five Red Dawn members?" Batman asked.

"I scanned, um, let's see, um," Flash stammered. "One?"

"One?" Green Lantern snapped. "All that running around and you only got one? I assume it was your new friend, Blaze."

"Actually, it was that little tank on legs," Flash explained, pulling the tiny DNA scanner from his belt. "Right after I scanned her I met Blaze, and . . . I guess I kind of forgot about the whole scanning thing."

"Sometimes . . ." Green Lantern sighed, looking at Flash and shaking his head. He wondered how someone with such great ability could be so irresponsible.

"One may be all we need," Batman announced. "Download the readings."

"Sure thing," Flash responded, glad to turn the focus away from his failure. He knew Green Lantern was right, and he should have been more professional on his mission, but meeting Blaze had turned his already hyperspeed mind upside down, and he had quickly lost track of a pesky little detail like getting DNA readings.

Flash slid the small scanner into a slot on the Watchtower's main computer. The information was downloaded via satellite link to the Batcomputer, deep in the mysterious, hidden Batcave.

Batman cross-referenced the data with his vast catalog of the super heroes and villains he and the others had encountered over the years. "No match to any known superpowered individual," the Dark Knight announced after a few minutes. "Which makes sense if the files on Red Dawn are true."

"Can you use the Watchtower's DNA satellite uplink to search Earth for their exact location?" Green Lantern asked, referring to a device that Batman had built into the Watchtower. Given a good enough DNA sample of any individual, Batman could use the uplink to pinpoint that person's location to within a few square miles.

"No," Batman replied, scowling. "A scan won't work well. Physical DNA samples work best. I've found a faint match somewhere in the Ural Mountains, but that's the best I can do."

"That's not surprising," Wonder Woman said. The Amazon Princess was well acquainted with the ways of warriors. "The cryogenic chamber where they were frozen is as close to a home as they have probably ever known. It is natural for warriors to seek shelter in a place of comfort following a defeat."

"That chamber might give us clues about Kolnikov's whereabouts," Batman pointed out.

"Were you able to learn what it is they want?" Green Lantern asked Wonder Woman.

"They think that Russia has been conquered by the United States," Wonder Woman explained.

"These guys think the Cold War is still going on," Flash explained. "They resent the fact that we got all the glory for saving the nuclear reactor, and they're hot to be accepted as heroes to the Russian people."

"It's hard to believe that they couldn't have researched the events of the last twenty years," Batman pointed out.

"Apparently, they think that the end of the Cold War and the friendship between the United States and Russia is some kind of lie or U.S. propaganda trick," Wonder Woman pointed out.

"I don't think Blaze completely buys that it's all a big fake," Flash added.

"And what is that based on?" Green Lantern asked.

"I'm not sure," Flash replied. "I just got the feeling that she had her doubts that we were all some big bad meanies they had to fight. If I could just see her again, I'm sure I could talk sense to her."

"That would be a first," Green Lantern said under his breath.

"I heard that!" Flash replied; then he turned to the monitor and directed his conversation to Batman. "I would like to head back to the Urals. Using the DNA reading I got, I could search the area until I find them."

"That mountain range is two thousand miles long," Batman reminded everyone.

"Exactly," Flash replied. "And who could search it faster than me?"

"He's right," Green Lantern agreed.

Flash shot him a look. *He's thinks I'm right? I should note the date and time!*

"This needs to be a mission of stealth," the Emerald Warrior explained. "A single operative would have the best chance of finding a clue about the general's location. If a bunch of us show up, it would just provoke another messy confrontation, not to mention additional diplomatic consequences. With Superman occupied trying to calm down the diplomats, Flash is our best bet for speed and stealth. If he's careful!" This last remark was aimed directly at Flash, who nodded, then rolled his eyes when Green Lantern turned away.

"If you find them, how will you get into the chamber?" Batman asked.

"I've been practicing a special technique," Flash explained. "I've been working on vibrating the molecules of my body so fast that they blend with those of an object—say the solid rock of a mountain—moving around the molecules of the object, letting me pass right through it."

"Have you ever actually done this?" Batman asked.

"Well, sort of. . . . I mean, um," Flash stammered. "No, not really. But I'm sure I can do it."

"Maybe I should go with you and cut our way in with my ring," Green Lantern suggested.

"Or I could tear open any door we encounter," Wonder Woman offered.

"Well, either of those choices would certainly keep our mission a surprise," Flash said sarcastically. "Why don't we just blast our way in with dynamite, shouting 'We're here and we're looking for clues!'"

"If J'onn were here, he could turn semitransparent and get in without being noticed," Batman said.

"Excuse me," Flash said, unable to mask the irritation in his voice. "I can do this. While it's flattering being everybody's last choice, trust me. I can handle it."

Batman, Green Lantern, and Wonder Woman agreed. Then Green Lantern helped outfit Flash with a special comm link that they attached to his belt.

"This communications device can send both voice and data transmissions," Batman explained. "It's linked to the Batcomputer and to the Watchtower's main computer. Stay in touch."

"Good luck," Wonder Woman said, smiling.

"Stay focused on the mission, hotshot," Green Lantern added.

"Like a dog chasing a stick, pal," Flash said. Then he boarded the *Javelin-7* for the return trip to Earth.

During the short shuttle run, Flash read the file on Red Dawn that Batman had quickly assembled for him. It included the names of the team members and brief descriptions of their powers.

When he got to the file on Blaze, he read the dossier over and over, thinking about how exciting it had been to meet her, even if it was in the thick of battle.

As the *Javelin-7* approached a flat landing area not far from the rugged Ural Mountains, the Flash wondered whether the exhilaration he was feeling was simple nervousness about his coming mission, or anticipation of the possibility of seeing Blaze again.

CHAPTER 8

Blaze paced nervously around the cryogenic laboratory deep in the Ural Mountains. The hours since their hasty retreat from Mount Rushmore and their return to the lab had been filled with anxiety and indecision for the confused speedster.

As the rockslide had struck, Blaze zoomed back to Red Fury, who had slipped into unconsciousness following his battle with Wonder Woman. Sinew arrived next. When she had seen her fallen comrade, she lifted him onto her shoulder, then ran from the gorge.

Blaze had then helped Beacon and Gray Heron get to their feet. The clouds of dust from the tumbling rocks had provided the cover that Red Dawn needed to slip from the area and head back to Russia. With

their leader down, they had seen no point in continuing the battle. And so, mustering all their remaining
strength, they'd fled.

As Blaze had raced back across the sea, she'd felt
very confused. For the first time since reawakening,
doubt crept into her mind. Flash's words about the
U.S. and Soviet Union somehow rang true. She could
not decide if she felt this way because she was intrigued by the Scarlet Speedster, or because the
Justice League hadn't launched an all-out attack on
Red Dawn at Mount Rushmore. If they were indeed enemies, why wouldn't they have sent the entire team to
eliminate Red Dawn with a full show of their might?

Blaze now stopped her pacing and stared down at the
still-unconscious form of Red Fury. He was sprawled
out on one of the steel tables in the lab's central room.
According to Beacon and Gray Heron, who had been
closest to Red Fury during his battle, the Amazon had
done nothing to cause their leader's sudden weakness.
They were at a loss to explain his collapse.

The sight of this huge muscular figure slumped
helplessly on the lab table made Blaze feel even more
unsure of the future. *What do we do if Red Fury
doesn't recover?* she worried.

On a television monitor in the control room, a

reporter blared on about Red Dawn, the battle at Mount Rushmore, and deteriorating U.S.-Russian relations.

The whole world knows about us now, she thought. *How long will it be before they find our little sanctuary here?*

Blaze's racing thoughts were interrupted by a sudden movement on the lab table. Red Fury stirred and groaned, then opened his eyes and sat up abruptly.

"Why am I back here?" he asked, his voice sounding once again firm and commanding as strength returned to his body. Not waiting for an answer, he jumped from the table and hurried into the main control room, followed closely by Blaze.

In the control room, Beacon was busy at the lab's computer, trying to access the files of the scientists who had created project Red Dawn. He was searching for clues about the mysterious illness that had come upon Red Fury so suddenly in the midst of battle.

"It is good to see you awake again," Sinew said, clasping Red Fury's shoulder firmly.

"How do you feel?" Gray Heron asked.

"I'm fine," Red Fury replied, waving his hand as if pushing the question away. "Tell me what happened back there."

Taking turns, Sinew, Gray Heron, and Blaze filled

Red Fury in on the sudden end of the battle at Mount Rushmore.

"When Beacon saw you go down, he destroyed an outcropping, causing a rockslide," Blaze explained. "I believe that the two Justice League members escaped. We then took the opportunity to retreat until we could understand what happened to you. What do you recall exactly?"

"It came from out of nowhere," Red Fury replied. "I felt weak, then very warm and dizzy. The Amazon shoved me easily to the ground, then placed her golden rope around me. For a few moments I felt compelled to speak only the truth, though I can't remember what I said. The next thing I knew I was waking up here."

"I may have found something useful," Beacon announced, looking up from the monitor for the first time in hours. "I've managed to access Dr. Pushkin's private files. As I told you before, unfortunately, some of the files were damaged when you smashed the control panel. I've got an audio file, made around the time of our cryogenic freezing. It appears to be incomplete, but here's what I've got."

The five members of Red Dawn listened intently as Dr. Pushkin's voice crackled over the control room's speakers.

"*. . . soon after awakening, in order to maintain the integrity of their genetic structures.*"

Then the speakers went silent.

"That's it?" Red Fury raged. "That's all there is?"

"As I said," Beacon explained calmly. "The files were damaged." He played the tiny snippet of speech again and again, but its meaning was no more clear than it had been the first time.

"I believe he was talking about us," Blaze concluded. "It appears that something had to be done after we came out of cryogenic freeze in order maintain our genetic integrity."

"Perhaps that explains what happened to you," Gray Heron offered up to Red Fury. "Maybe your genetic structure is starting to break down."

"Will this happen to all of us?" Blaze wondered aloud.

"Dr. Pushkin is the only one who knows what needs to be done in order to stabilize our genetic makeup," Sinew pointed out. "But he is dead."

"*. . . soon after awakening, in order to maintain the integrity of their genetic structures,*" Dr. Pushkin's voice sounded again, like an echo from the grave. This time, however, the recording continued and a second voice came through the speakers.

"Fine, fine. Spare me the technical details and just get on with it!"

"General Kolnikov!" Red Fury exclaimed. The sound of the general's voice offered a glimpse of hope. "He will know what must be done to stabilize our genetic structures. It is now imperative that we find him."

"But how?" asked Gray Heron. Then he suddenly collapsed to the floor, gasping for breath.

"Heron!" Blaze shouted as she and Sinew rushed to his side.

Gray Heron's breathing returned to normal, and he slipped into a deep sleep.

"Are we just going to wait here until each one of us is affected by this genetic breakdown?" Blaze asked, a bit more forcefully than she would have liked.

"That may not be necessary," Beacon announced, having uncovered another of Pushkin's files.

While Sinew carried Gray Heron to a lab table, Blaze and Red Fury peered over Beacon's shoulder.

"It appears that Dr. Pushkin set up a second, smaller cryogenic lab in addition to this one," Beacon explained. "It's not far from here, and it may hold some answers. It's at least worth investigating."

"A second lab," Red Fury repeated, intrigued.

"I'll investigate it," Blaze volunteered. "Speed and stealth are of the utmost importance. We must find this lab before the rest of us become too weak to act. And with the media buzzing about Red Dawn, the fewer of us out in public, the better."

Red Fury stared at Blaze for a moment. "Go then, and find that second lab," he ordered. He then yanked a small black rectangular box from his belt and handed it to her. "This is the signal device we use to open the entrance to this lab. It may be helpful in locating and opening Pushkin's second facility."

Blaze nodded and took the device, then sat down next to Beacon, who shared what he had found about the second lab. While its exact location was not clear, Blaze got a pretty good idea of where to begin her search. With a quick glance back at Gray Heron, she turned and sped from the laboratory.

Flash raced up the jagged peaks, then down into the deep valleys of the windswept Ural Mountains. In his hand he grasped a small scanner that had been programmed to search for the DNA imprint of Sinew.

The comm link on his belt, which was tied into the usual one he wore in his ear, kept him in constant contact with Batman in the Batcave, and Green Lantern and Wonder Woman on the Watchtower.

"Five hundred miles down, fifteen hundred to go," Flash reported as he sped along. "No sign of the Russian ballerina or of the secret lab."

"Keep us posted," Wonder Woman said through the comm link.

"You guys'll be the first to know," Flash replied.

As he continued his high-speed search, his thoughts turned back to Blaze. *I know I'm supposed to be looking for the lab and clues about General What's His Face, but I can't help thinking that if I could just talk with Blaze again, I could convince her that we're not enemies.*

Flash sighed deeply.

Figures, with my luck, that I meet someone I really like, and I can tell she likes me, and she turns out to be a defrosted relic from the Cold War. But hey, if it wasn't tough and complicated, it just wouldn't be any fun at—

Flash's thoughts were interrupted by his DNA scanner.

—deepdeeepdeepdeeep—

"No more calls, please," he said, slowing to a stop. "We have a winner!"

"I see it," Batman replied. The information from the

DNA scanner was transmitted by the comm link's data port to a readout on the Batcomputer. "Looks like you found your match."

Flash recovered the ground he had just raced across, tightening the arc of his path, following the strength of the scanner's signal to narrow in on the exact location of Sinew—and the cryogenic lab.

"The reading seems to max out right here," Flash reported, moving the scanner across a curved section of rock extending up from the narrow plateau on which he stood.

"Any sign of a door?" Green Lantern asked.

Flash ran his gloved finger along the surface of the rock where the DNA reading was the strongest. "No such luck," he said. "No door, no window, no 'welcome to the secret lab' sign. Looks like they are not too fond of visitors. I'm going to have to do this the hard way."

"Good luck, hotshot," said Green Lantern. "You can do this."

"Thanks, pal," Flash replied. For as much as Flash and Green Lantern sometimes clashed over style, methods, and personality, Flash had nothing but respect for the Emerald Warrior's knowledge and experience. His words of encouragement meant a great deal to the Scarlet Speedster.

Flash switched off the DNA scanner and hooked it onto his belt. Then he shut off his comm link. He knew that the slightest disturbance or interruption could spell disaster.

Slowly the Flash brought his hands together in front of his face and took a deep, even breath. Using the meditation techniques J'onn had taught him, Flash concentrated on slowing his thoughts and focusing all his power on the task at hand.

Steady, he thought, *easy, focus. Focus.* Placing his palms flat against the smooth rock wall, the Flash eased his body forward until his chest and legs also pressed against the hard surface.

Breathing steadily, uniformly, Flash felt his heart rate slow. He concentrated all his tremendous power of speed not as he usually did—on moving his legs as quickly as possible—but rather on accelerating the individual molecules of his body so that they moved faster and faster.

That's it, he thought as an odd numbness spread through his body. He had never actually achieved the feat of vibrating through a solid object. He had lived through the experience in his meditations and had seen his mentor, Barry Allen, perform the feat countless times. Yet somehow he knew that he was doing it correctly, that this unfamiliar feeling coursing through his veins meant that he was on the right track.

The numbness in his body gave way to a fluid sensation, and he felt himself moving forward, as if through a thick liquid rather than through solid rock. The molecules of his body spread in their accelerated orbit, moving around and past those of the rock.

Flash moved forward at an excruciatingly slow pace, repeating the simple word in his mind, *focus, focus,* just as J'onn had taught him during their exercises together. In the back of his mind, Flash knew that if he lost concentration or pushed his journey too quickly, his own molecules could very easily end up fused with those of the rock, leaving him trapped in the side of this mountain forever.

This thought caused a tiny knot of panic to form deep in the outer regions of his consciousness, but he pushed the thought down, repeating, *focus, focus,* as he moved further ahead.

The journey continued, one painfully slow step at a time, for what seemed like days to Flash, but in reality was only minutes. Through no conscious decision, his pace suddenly picked up. The feeling had shifted from one of walking through molasses to that of gliding through a deep pool of water. The steps came more easily now, and Flash fought hard to hold back his excitement at his own success.

And then he was through.

The liquid sensation shifted back to the numbness in his body, and the solid brown that had filled his field of vision gave way to patches of color as he stepped through the thick wall and into Red Dawn's secret laboratory.

Fortunately for the Flash, he emerged at a point some distance from the lab's main area and control room. Leaning against the wall, he caught his breath. *I made it!* he thought as feeling flowed back into his limbs and his vision returned to normal. Glancing around, he saw no one, but he heard noises from down a corridor.

He switched his comm link back on. "I'm in," he whispered.

Flash could hear sighs of relief from his friends in the Watchtower and the Batcave.

"You okay?" Green Lantern asked.

"Never better, pal," Flash whispered. "I'm going to take a peek around."

Feeling his energy restored, Flash raced down the corridor at blinding speed, exhilarated not only by his achievement, but by the realization of how much easier it was to move his legs at superspeed than it had been to move his individual molecules.

Flash entered the lab's main chamber, running around its perimeter. Then he sped in and out of the control room, where Beacon sat at the main computer with Red Fury looking over his shoulder. Flash was now moving faster than the eyes of Red Dawn could follow. It was as if he were invisible to them, which was precisely what he had in mind.

As he streaked through the main room, Flash spotted Gray Heron and Sinew, each lying on a separate steel lab table, apparently unconscious. There was no sign of Blaze anywhere.

Having read of Red Fury's abilities, Flash feared that even a whisper might be detected by his enhanced hearing, so he brought his teammates up to speed on the situation in the lab via a Morse code signal transmitted through his comm link. He repeated his unseen journey around the main room and through the control room again and again, several times a second.

"See if you can locate a data port in the control room's main computer," Batman advised, using the same coded transmission. "Place the comm link's data probe into the port. That should relay all the system's files back here to me."

On his next pass through the control room, Flash slipped the probe into the computer. Two passes later, Batman signaled that all the files had been downloaded. On his next trip through the room, Flash snatched the probe from the console, far too fast for Beacon or Red Fury to notice.

While Flash kept running, Batman quickly analyzed this new data. Among all the information he received, the existence of Dr. Pushkin's second cryogenic lab instantly leapt out at the Dark Knight.

"That's the next logical place to search," Batman signaled. "You work on getting out of there, while I try to pinpoint the exact location of the second lab from these files."

Flash signaled his agreement, then headed back down the corridor to the spot where he had entered the lab, accidentally tripping an alarm in the process.

BREEP! BREEP! BREEP!

An intruder defense system activated, setting off an earsplitting alert. Thick panels of metal slid from the ceiling, dropping down along all the walls, sealing the lab shut.

"They know I'm here!" Flash shouted into the comm link, no longer concerned about being heard. "And I'm trapped!"

CHAPTER 9

"Show yourself, intruder!" Red Fury blustered as he and Beacon raced into the lab's main room. "I don't know how you got in, but there is no way out."

Flash continued circling the steel-encased perimeter of the lab at top speed, still unseen by Red Fury or Beacon. He was certain, having successfully vibrated through the rock, that he could do the same with the metal panels. However, he didn't think that his adversaries would give him the opportunity to prepare himself for the task, which required him to be stationary, and also took tremendous concentration.

Flash filled his teammates in on the situation in the lab. "If I stop long enough to get myself ready to vibrate back out of here, I'll be an easy target for one of

Beacon's power blasts," he explained. "So I'm open to any suggestions, gang!"

"Working on it," Batman replied. In the Batcave, the Dark Knight continued searching the files he had received earlier.

At that moment, Sinew stirred, then sat upright. She felt her strength returning and quickly noticed the steel plates that now covered the lab's walls. "What's going on?" she asked, lifting herself off the table and standing. She glanced over at the still-unconscious form of Gray Heron.

"Intruder," Beacon explained. "One, however, that we can't see."

Oh, great, Flash thought as he kept running. *Now another one's awake, which means if I stop, it's three against one.*

"Flash, I've got something," came the message from Batman. "I've found the computer codes that will raise the metal plates and open the door. But you're going to have to stop long enough to punch the codes in manually."

"Thanks, Bats," Flash replied. "Send them along. I'll take it from here."

Flash saw a blinking light on his comm link and knew that Batman was transmitting the necessary codes he would need to make his escape. "Got 'em!" he acknowledged. "Now I just need a little diversion."

As he reached the back of the lab's main area for the fourth time that second, Flash overturned the two lab tables farthest from the control room. To the members of Red Dawn, the tables seemed to spin into the air under their own power, then crash to the floor with a chiming metallic clang.

"There!" Red Fury shouted. "The intruder has revealed himself!"

Red Fury flew swiftly toward the back of the main room, followed by Sinew and Beacon.

Flash reached the computer in the empty control room and stopped suddenly. *Just need a second or two,* he thought, quickly punching a code sequence into the keyboard.

The steel plates surrounding the lab suddenly slipped up into the ceiling, and the three members of Red Dawn spun around, looking into the control room.

"There he is!" Sinew cried, pointing, as they raced toward the intruder. "One of the Justice League members we battled at the monument has somehow found his way here!"

"And now, ladies and gentlemen, if I may be so bold," Flash quipped, "he's going to find his way back out!"

ZZZZAATTT! KA-RASH!!

Beacon fired a blast of energy from his yellow gemstone. The searing beam traveled the length of the main room, shattering the thick double-glass window.

The impact slammed Flash into the far wall. He dropped to the floor as shards of glass rained down on him. Struggling to his feet, he stumbled back to the keyboard and punched in the second code. A section of the rock wall slid open, revealing daylight. Then he hurried to the doorway just as Red Fury landed in the opening.

"You'll have to get past me first!" Red Fury boasted, hands on hips, legs spread wide. He braced himself, anticipating an attempt by the Flash to ram his way past.

Flash put on a burst of speed, and just as he reached the imposing figure in the doorway, he squatted and dove through Red Fury's open legs. Somersaulting onto the rocky ledge just outside the opening, the Scarlet Speedster rolled to his feet.

"Thanks," he said as Red Fury turned in shock. "It's been great. I haven't had so much fun since my last root canal."

As Flash zoomed away, he spoke into the comm link. "I made it out of there," he reported.

"I've managed to narrow down the search area for the second lab, based on Pushkin's files," Batman replied. "It should be along the main mountain road, probably within about five miles of the first lab. Set your scanner to pick up any kind of technology. That should help you pinpoint the exact location."

"I'll let you know when I find it," Flash said. Then he switched off the comm link and began his search.

Blaze streaked along the winding narrow road that led through the mountains. On her left, the Urals rose toward the clouds. Glancing to her right, Blaze saw a sheer drop into misty darkness below. In her hand she grasped the signal device Red Fury had given her. Sweeping the small rectangular box back and forth across the face of the mountain, Blaze hoped that the frequency used to gain access to the main cryogenic lab would match that of the second facility.

Her mind raced along, moving as fast as her feet.

She knew what her mission was: to search the second lab in the hope that some clue there might lead them to General Kolnikov. Finding the general seemed to be the only hope Red Dawn had of surviving. It was clear to her now that some part of the cryogenic process had been left out during their unexpected awakening, and that this oversight had potentially deadly consequences.

Blaze worried about how long it would be before the condition that had struck Red Fury and then Gray Heron would affect her. She felt as if she were a walking time bomb, set to go off at an unknown moment.

And then there were her growing doubts about all that the others seemed to accept easily. The more she saw of this world, the harder it was for her to believe that the United States could have faked so much history and executed such an all-encompassing propaganda campaign. Yet she was hesitant to betray Red Fury. Her sense of duty, embedded in her genetic makeup, was still strong.

Finally, Blaze's thoughts turned to the Flash. Speeding along the gravely road, she realized that this was the first time since the battle at Mount Rushmore that she had had a moment to reflect on this strange man who so intrigued her. In the quiet solitude of her high-speed search, images of the crimson-clad hero filled her mind.

She thought about how exhilarating it had felt to

engage in an edgy competition with someone who could keep up with her speed. Although her first reaction had been not to trust him, her gut told her something different.

His wise-guy wit appealed to her, and trading barbs had been as exciting as their chase around the granite cliffs in South Dakota. Plus, there was something that was just plain fun about the guy. It went against all her training and made her feel a bit guilty, but when she was really being honest with herself, Blaze realized that she liked him.

bripp bripp bripp bripp . . .

Blaze's soul searching was suddenly interrupted by a low chirping from the signal device. She slowed to a halt, then deliberately retraced her last few steps, waving the box along the length of wall she had just passed.

BRIPP! BRIPP! BRIPP! BRIPP! . . .

The device beeped loudly now as she moved it back and forth over a small section of rock. Punching in the code that was used to open the secret door at the main lab, Blaze held her breath and waited. A few seconds later a small section of the mountain parted, opening into a narrow doorway.

Blaze sighed with relief. *I guess Dr. Pushkin saw no*

need to change the entry code for his second lab, since
apparently none of his colleagues knew it even existed,
she thought, stepping toward the dark entryway.

"You just saved me an awful lot of hard work," said a
voice from behind her. "How can I possibly thank you?"

Spinning around, Blaze found herself face to face
with the Flash.

"You!" she cried, startled at his silent, unexpected arrival, and also a bit embarrassed that she had just been
thinking about him. "How did you find this place?"

"Long story," Flash replied. "And I think we're both
short on time. Especially you."

Blaze stared at him in tight-lipped silence. She realized that the moment had come when she had to
make her choice, either to fight Flash or work with
him to find a solution to Red Dawn's deadly dilemma.

"I just left the other lab," Flash said, seeing the
doubt and confusion on her face. "What's going on
with your buddies back there? Two of them looked as
if they weren't even going to make it through the next
hour. Is the same thing going to happen to you? Is
that why you're here, searching for answers?"

Blaze nodded, then turned away.

"How many times do we have to tell you, the Cold War
is over," he said gently, seeing that she was struggling

with what to do next. "We're not enemies, despite your training and what that gruesome twosome on steroids back there may say. We're on the same side. In fact, as a show of good faith, I'll even tell you why *I'm* here."

Blaze looked right at him.

"I'm trying to figure out where the general who started project Red Dawn is," Flash explained. "The Justice League believes that maybe he can convince all of you that we are telling the truth."

"I, too, seek General Kolnikov," Blaze admitted. "Red Dawn thinks he knows what is happening to us, and how to stop it."

"So what do we do, Blaze?" Flash said, placing his arms down by his side and jutting out his chin. "You want to take your best shot? You want to knock me out and do this alone? Go ahead. I won't stop you."

Blaze looked down at the ground and shook her head. "No," she said. "I don't want to hurt you."

"That's great news," Flash replied. "Because I don't want to hurt you either."

"What do you propose we do?" she asked.

"How about we work together, since we're both looking for the same guy?" he suggested. "Flash and Blaze, 'the Fastest Man and Woman Alive.' Got a nice ring to it, don't you think?"

"I think 'Blaze and Flash' sounds better," she replied, smiling for the first time in a very long while.

"Hey, who am I to quibble about details?" Flash asked. Then he gestured to the open entrance before them. "After you."

Blaze stepped into the lab, followed closely by Flash.

The two walked slowly in total darkness through a series of branching tunnels.

"You didn't bring a flashlight by any chance, did you?" Flash asked as they felt their way along the tunnel walls.

"*You're* the guy named 'Flash,'" Blaze shot back. "Shouldn't *you* have one?"

"Hey," Flash said as they reached a short, wide tunnel, "I make the bad jokes around here."

At the end of the last tunnel, Blaze's hand ran across a round knob. "I found something," she announced. When Blaze pressed the circular switch, lights flared on ahead of them.

Flash saw that the short tunnel opened into a small laboratory set up like a miniature version of the cryogenic lab he had just escaped from. A small control room packed with equipment sat off a tiny central area. A door on the far side resembled the one leading to the cryogenic freezing chamber in the other lab, only smaller.

"I've got some friends who can help us," Flash said to Blaze, switching on his comm link.

Blaze raised her eyebrows in surprise.

"Batman? Green Lantern? Wonder Woman?" Flash spoke into the comm link. "You guys still there?"

"We're here," Green Lantern replied. "Where are *you*?"

"We're in the second lab," Flash reported.

"Did you vibrate through the wall again?" Green Lantern asked.

"Not necessary," Flash said into the comm link. "The door was open."

"'We'?" Wonder Woman asked.

"Blaze is here with me," Flash said casually. "She says hi," he added, winking at her.

"Blaze!" Green Lantern shouted.

"Relax, GL," Flash said. "She's on our side now. In fact, she's the one who let me into this place."

"Uh-huh," Green Lantern muttered skeptically.

"Is the power to the cryogenic freezing chamber on?" Batman asked.

"Why would it be on, unless—whoa!" Flash exclaimed. "I get your point. I'll check."

Flash raced into the cramped control room, followed by Blaze. "Vibrate through the wall?" she asked, puzzled.

Flash smiled as he searched the control room's console. "It's tons of fun," he said. "I'll teach you how sometime."

A small red light just above the computer's monitor blinked steadily. A label beneath it said CRYOGENICS.

"Looks like it's still working," Flash reported.

"It must be on a different power grid than the nuclear reactor and the first lab," Green Lantern said.

"Stop me if I'm wrong, here," Flash said into his comm link. "But this means that someone is alive, frozen in that cryogenic chamber!"

"Scan the handle on the door to the chamber, see if you can get some prints," Batman said calmly.

"I'll see if I can get the computer system up and running," Blaze said, sitting down at the control panel.

Flash streaked across the lab's central area to the chamber's door. Switching the comm link into its data-scan mode, he swept the device across the handle. The scanner beeped, indicating a positive "finding" of prints.

"I read two sets of prints," the Dark Knight said a few seconds later. "I'm checking the KGB files for a match."

Flash zoomed back to the control room.

"I've got the computer system up and running," Blaze

reported. "According to the readings, there is one person in the chamber, in perfect cryogenic hibernation."

"I've got a match for both prints," Batman announced over the comm link. "One set is Pushkin's. No surprise there. The other belongs to General Kolnikov."

"What!" exclaimed Blaze. "Kolnikov, here?"

"I can't figure out how or why," Batman continued. "But it's a good bet the general's in that chamber."

"Can you open it?" Flash asked Blaze.

Pulling up the files associated with the freeze chamber, Blaze found a complex coded password system in place. "No," she said bitterly. "The chamber can only be opened using a sophisticated series of codes and passwords."

"Leave it to the Soviets," said Flash. "No offense," he added quickly.

"It could take years to break these codes," Blaze said, sighing.

"That won't be necessary," said a deep voice from the entryway.

Flash and Blaze looked up in shock as Red Fury, Sinew, and Beacon stepped into the lab's central area.

CHAPTER 10

Blaze sped to Red Fury's side.

"Listen, please," she pleaded, speaking rapidly. "You're wrong about them. Flash has been helping me. We've found General Kolnikov. The Justice League wants to help us overcome our genetic instability."

"Yes," Red Fury grumbled. "We overheard quite a bit. So, the general is frozen in that chamber. But why would your boyfriend there want to help? He wants to find Kolnikov to gain control of Red Dawn, not to assist us. Don't think I didn't notice you two playing tag at Mount Rushmore, and the recent looks of doubt on your face. You've been staring at the television watching news reports mournfully, believing every word of the propaganda!"

"But it's not propaganda!" Blaze shouted back. "It's the truth!"

"The truth," Red Fury repeated, "is that you are a traitor and you will now pay the price for your treachery!"

Red Fury snatched the signal device from Blaze's belt. He entered the control code, and the door to the lab slid shut with a faint grinding sound that drifted down the maze of entryway tunnels.

"A very handy tool," he said, slipping the small black box onto his belt. "In addition to opening doors, it also contains a homing signal, with which we were able to follow you.

"Beacon, eliminate them! Sinew, come with me. It's time to get reacquainted with the general!"

Beacon fired an energy blast from his gemstone right at Blaze. She took off just as the searing jolt of yellow energy struck a lab table, melting it into a puddle of molten slag.

"Beacon, you've got to listen," Blaze pleaded as she sped around the outside of the room. "Our training no longer applies. The world has changed, and we must change too!"

Beacon looked right at Blaze. "You choose to believe *him*?" he asked, pointing at the Flash.

Flash ran up behind Beacon. "Listen, pal," he began. "You're awfully sure of yourself for a guy who's been asleep for twenty years."

Beacon whirled and fired another blast at Flash. The Scarlet Speedster dodged the energy beam, the streaking yellow bolt exploding against the far wall of the central area, spraying rocks and debris across the tiny room.

"You'll never catch us, Beacon," Flash said, zigzagging around the lab. "You didn't even see me at the other lab until I stopped. Don't you think I could have done some damage to you back there if I'd wanted to? Doesn't that tell you anything?"

Beacon paused to think about what Flash said. Doubt crept into his mind, but his loyalty to Red Fury was fierce, and the thought of turning on his leader was more than he could handle.

Flash and Blaze kept moving at speeds too fast for Beacon to pin them down.

Across the central room, Red Fury and Sinew each grabbed one side of the thick steel door that sealed the cryogenic freezing chamber.

"Together now," Red Fury said.

With a tremendous outpouring of sheer physical might, the two strongest members of Red Dawn yanked the door from its hinges. It sprung loose with a wrenching crunch, and they tossed it aside. The massive hunk of twisted metal clanged to the floor, bouncing end over end, finally coming to rest near the control room.

Clouds of crystalline mist billowed from the chamber. Within moments, groaning and stirring could be heard from inside. Then a tall, thin man with red hair and a gray-speckled goatee stepped from the chamber. The man's long white lab coat was wrinkled, and he stumbled forward with a dazed look in his eyes.

"Dr. Pushkin!" Red Fury exclaimed.

"But how can this be?" cried Sinew.

At Red Fury's exclamation, Beacon turned toward the chamber. Flash and Blaze stopped running and stared in disbelief.

Dr. Pushkin leaned against the side of the chamber door, holding himself up. He looked pale and tired as he squinted in the lab's bright lights. "Where am I?" he asked weakly.

"Dead, from all the historical reports," replied Red Fury. "A car crash, I believe."

"Red Fury, Sinew, why have you been revived?" Dr. Pushkin asked. "Why am I—Oh, yes. Now I remember."

"We are early in the twenty-first century," Red Fury explained. "Red Dawn was revived accidentally. But tell us, how did you come to be locked in your own cryogenic chamber?"

Dr. Pushkin eased himself into a sitting position on the floor. He was simply too weak to remain standing. When he spoke, it was with a thin, frail voice. "I had dreams of gaining control of Red Dawn," he began, the memories pouring back. "I planned to take the power away from General Kolnikov. With that in mind, I lured him here immediately after you five were placed into cryogenic freeze. A struggle ensued, which I lost. Kolnikov overpowered me and shoved me into the chamber. I had programmed it to seal automatically upon entry. And so I was trapped for—what did you say?—several decades, it appears."

Pushkin looked around the lab, his vision blurry. Waves of nausea wracked his body, followed by intense pain in all his joints. His face turned bright red and he began sweating profusely. His plan had failed, and twenty years of his life had just vanished in what felt to him like an instant.

"Where is General Kolnikov?" he asked weakly.

"We were hoping you could tell us," Sinew replied.

Blaze raced up to Dr. Pushkin and knelt down

beside him. "Never mind the general," she said impatiently. "Dr. Pushkin can tell us what we need to know!"

She looked into the doctor's glassy eyes. He groaned and clutched his stomach, his face a twisted mask of torment. "Dr. Pushkin," she said softly. "Can you tell us what we need to do in order to stabilize our genetic integrity? Something was left out when we were revived, and we've all been suffering."

Pushkin stared up at Blaze with sadness and confusion in his eyes, like a man desperate to say something, but unable to form the words. He mumbled incoherently, then screamed in agony, tumbling over, sprawling onto the floor, writhing in pain.

Blaze stood up and watched with the others as Pushkin's face lost its form, his skin dropping away in clumps that splattered onto the floor. His features dripped down his skull, like a candle melting. Then his bones snapped audibly and his blood flowed freely, spreading in a sickly crimson pool.

It was all over in a few moments. Dr. Pushkin was gone.

"Is that the fate that awaits the rest of us?" Blaze asked angrily. "One by one we dissolve into a pool of blood, dying a horrible death? It took only moments for his genetic failure to take place. For some reason we have been given more time, but how much more?"

The Flash sped to her side. "Which is why we must work together to find the general," he said. "He's your last hope."

"The newspaper reports said Pushkin died in a car crash," Red Fury shouted. "Perhaps it was Kolnikov who died in that crash. Which leaves us with no hope. This is your fault, Justice Leaguer. You awakened us, and you must pay the price for our destruction!"

Chaos suddenly broke loose in the tiny lab.

As Sinew leapt at Flash, he dove out of the way, somersaulting, then quickly regained his feet. Sinew slammed into the opposite wall, shaking the cavern, sending dust and rocks cascading down from the ceiling.

Seeing that there would be no reasoning with her teammates, Blaze dashed across the room as Red Fury unleashed twin heat beams from his eyes. They narrowly missed Blaze and, instead, ignited a control panel. Sparks burst from the equipment, followed by thick white smoke, then orange flames that quickly spread as Blaze continued on her high-speed dash through the lab.

As Flash also did his best to stay in constant motion, his comm link beeped. It was Batman signaling him.

"Flash," the Dark Knight said. "Get me the handle from the door to the cryogenic chamber."

"I'm a bit busy here, Bats," Flash replied, speeding out of the way of a searing burst of heat vision from Red Fury.

"It's important!" Batman replied sternly.

"Sure," Flash said. "I'll add it to my 'to do' list."

He made another sweep of the lab, keeping an eye on Blaze's situation, while he came up with a plan. Noticing Beacon following his movements, the Scarlet Speedster stopped right in front of the crumpled cryogenic chamber door that rested on the floor in a twisted heap of metal.

Beacon spotted Flash and fired a yellow gemstone blast. Not realizing that his teammate was about to attack, Red Fury took advantage of the Flash's standing still and dove at the Scarlet Speedster, tackling him just as Beacon's energy discharge struck the door.

THOOM!

The door shattered to bits from the force of the impact, scattering like shrapnel around the lab. Sinew dove for cover, and Blaze sped delicately out of the way of the flying metal shards.

Red Fury's body protected Flash from harm, but he now found himself in the iron grip of Red Dawn's leader. Flash rotated his body, spinning like a high-speed top, as Red Fury brought his massive arms together, attempting to tighten his grip. The force of his squeezing acted as a catapult, firing the rotating Flash from his arms like a whirling crimson spear.

Flash stopped spinning and landed on his feet, then he raced over to the shattered chamber door, reaching down and grabbing the handle, as smoke from the damaged control panel grew thicker and flames spread throughout the lab.

"We've got to get out of here, now!" he shouted to Blaze.

"How do we do that?" she asked, ducking swiftly to narrowly avoid a crushing blow from Sinew's powerful fist.

"Stay close," Flash replied. "And follow my lead."

The Flash sped down a tunnel, coming to a sudden halt next to the section of wall that had opened to allow them entry into the lab. *I sure hope this trick works twice,* he thought.

As if reading his mind, Beacon shot another energy burst toward Flash, who dashed away just as the beam tore a huge hole in the wall, exposing the darkening sky outside.

"Let's go!" Flash shouted, turning around in time to see Blaze collapse. Pressing hard on his heels to execute a sudden stop, the Scarlet Speedster shifted direction and swept back toward Blaze, catching her unconscious form just before it hit the ground.

Changing directions again, Flash sped through the newly blasted hole, racing away from the lab at top speed, clutching Blaze firmly in his arms.

"You did that intentionally!" Sinew railed, turning on Beacon, shouting in his face, and pointing an accusing finger. "You allowed him to use your power for his own purposes. You might as well leave with them, traitor!"

Beacon looked out through the hole in the wall and for a moment considered joining Flash and Blaze. Then his face suddenly turned bright red and he began to sweat. As he fell toward the floor, Red Fury stepped up and caught his yellow-clad teammate.

"Enough!" shouted Red Fury, hoisting Beacon onto his shoulder. "We must leave here while we still can, before fire consumes the entire facility, or we all collapse like Blaze and Beacon!"

Red Fury led the way out through the hole, carrying Beacon over his shoulder, holding him securely with one hand. His other arm wrapped firmly around Sinew's waist, he took to the air, flying back toward the main lab.

Below, a loud explosion rocked the mountainside. Looking back, Red Fury saw smoke and flames pour from the ruins of what had once been Dr. Pushkin's secret lab.

"Time grows short," Red Fury said. "I'm no longer certain of Beacon's loyalty either. But if the general is not found soon, it will not matter. We'll all suffer the same fate as Dr. Pushkin."

"But how can we possibly find him now?" Sinew asked.

"I took the liberty of planting a tiny homing device onto Flash's costume when I tackled him earlier," Red Fury explained. "We will let *him* lead us to the general."

CHAPTER 11

Flash sped through the Ural Mountains, retracing the five-hundred-mile trip back to the spot where he had left the *Javelin-7*. He hurried, each foot barely touching the ground before the other thrusted forward. Carrying Blaze, his concern for her grew with each step.

As he ran, he contacted Batman and the others, quickly filling them in on the events in the second lab, including the strange death of Dr. Pushkin and Blaze's current condition.

"I got that door handle for you, Batman," Flash reported as he approached the waiting space shuttle. "But Blaze is sick. We're heading back to the Watchtower. I hope you've got some good ideas about what to do next."

"Get up there as fast as you can," Batman replied. "Contact me when you arrive."

Reaching the shuttle, Flash swiftly but gently placed Blaze into the copilot's seat. Dropping the seatback down, he strapped her in for the short ride up to the Watchtower. As he looked down at her pale, haggard face, Flash realized how much she had come to mean to him in so short a time. He felt a strong connection to this fellow speed merchant who, if not for the nuclear accident, might have remained in hibernation forever. He could not bear the thought of losing her now.

Firing up the *Javelin-7*'s main engine, he blasted the shuttle into space.

During the trip, Flash noticed the color slowly returning to Blaze's face. She stirred, then her eyes fluttered open.

"Welcome back," he said, smiling. "You're aboard Justice League Airlines, flight number five. Your beverage service will be along any minute."

"What happened?" Blaze asked softly, feeling her strength start to return. "I remember a fire and . . . the next thing I knew, well, here I am."

"Your pal Beacon blasted a hole in the door," Flash exclaimed. "Of course, he was aiming at me. But I think he may have chosen to help us out. With Gray Heron still out of it, I get the feeling that only Red Fury and Sinew are still holding on to their Cold War issues. All that hardly seems to matter anymore, since it appears that if we don't get help for them soon, they're going to end up as small puddles of goo, like Pushkin back there."

As soon as he had said it, Flash realized that he'd made a mistake. Blaze grew tight-lipped and looked away.

Nice going, Einstein, he berated himself. *Blaze has just as much chance to end up as a big blob of genetic mush as any of the rest of them. Great show of compassion. Maybe you should have gone into nursing.*

His mind spun in ten directions at once, all of them focusing on just how stupid he felt about the remark.

"We're going to help you," he finally said, breaking the uncomfortable silence. "I'm not going to let you become—"

"A small puddle of goo?" she repeated, looking back at him. "Your confidence is overwhelming."

The rest of the trip passed in silence.

After docking, Flash and Blaze raced to the Watchtower's main observation deck, where they joined Green Lantern and Wonder Woman.

"You all know Blaze, I believe," Flash said, meeting the skeptical looks of his teammates with a shrug of his shoulders. "But we're in a bit of a hurry now, so we can save the formal introductions for later."

"You got that door handle?" Green Lantern asked.

"Right here," Flash replied, handing it over.

Green Lantern placed the jagged piece of metal into a scanning bay that was attached to the Watchtower's DNA satellite uplink. This sophisticated piece of equipment, designed by Batman, took DNA samples and created 3-D digital models of their genetic sequences.

Blaze looked around at the Justice League's headquarters and immediately felt uncomfortable. Despite having decided to work with Flash, and having come to the realization that Red Fury was wrong to cling to his old training, she still felt strange standing on the observation deck of the headquarters of her former enemies. She gazed out the long, curved window, looking down at the blue-green globe of Earth suspended in the velvet blackness of space.

"You appear to have recovered, Blaze," Wonder Woman said gently, sensing her unease.

"Yes," Blaze replied. "Thank you. It appears that the initial effects of our condition are temporary. My strength has returned, for now. But I fear the results of future incidents."

Lights flashed on the scanning bay. "You getting this, Batman?" Green Lantern asked as digital models of the DNA samples from the door handle were transmitted down to Earth.

"I'm getting it," Batman replied.

deep deep deep . . .

"That's it," Green Lantern said at the sound of a signal from the scanner. "The DNA analysis and transmission is complete."

"Got it," Batman replied. On a large monitor in the Batcave, Batman watched as two computer-generated images appeared. Each digital model showed a twisting ladder of genetic information unique to one human being. The ropelike strands of DNA sat side by side on the screen.

"There are definitely two individuals here," Batman reported. "They've got to be Pushkin and Kolnikov. I'll search for both."

With the Batcomputer already tied into the Watchtower's main system, Batman was easily able to operate the satellite uplink in order to search the Earth for matching DNA.

"The first one's come up negative," the Dark Knight reported after a few minutes.

"That must be Pushkin," Green Lantern concluded. "From the description of his death, I'd guess that his DNA got pretty scrambled. What about the next one?"

Blaze let out a sharp cry of pain, then stumbled backward. She fell toward Wonder Woman, who caught her and eased her gently to the floor.

"Blaze!" Flash cried, racing to her side and kneeling down next to her. Sweat dripped from her crimson face. Her eyes closed and her breathing grew shallow.

Fear washed over Flash, mixed with guilt over his "puddle of goo" remark. His mind jumped to an image of Blaze reduced to a mass of genetic liquid. He fought to clear the picture from his mind as he felt hope drain away.

"Get her to a bio table," Green Lantern shouted. "We'll monitor her life signs from here. Batman, how are you doing on that second scan?"

"Working on it," Batman replied evenly.

Flash lifted Blaze off the floor, cradling her gently in his arms. Dashing to the Watchtower's medical lab, he placed her unconscious form onto a bed that was hooked up to a bank of readouts above. The readings sprung to life as soon as Blaze's body touched the bed. Her heart beat slowly as her temperature rose. Her pulse was weak, and her blood pressure dropped steadily. Though he was no doctor, Flash knew what these readings meant. Blaze was dying.

He took Blaze's hand into his own. Grabbing a nearby washcloth, he dabbed at her forehead, mopping up sweat, which reappeared as soon as he removed the cloth.

He was going to lose her; he felt certain of that. And he felt helpless. This was one situation he couldn't joke his way out of. If only he had been smarter. If only he had been faster.

Flash felt a hand on his shoulder. Its firm but gentle grasp startled him slightly, but he knew who it was without even turning around. "Hey, Princess," he said, forcing a smile. "She looks pretty bad."

"Do not despair, my friend," Wonder Woman said softly. "There is still hope."

"Thanks, Diana," Flash said, looking up at the Amazon Princess, realizing what a valuable friend she had become.

The med-lab's com system beeped, sending Flash

speeding to a small speaker mounted on the wall. "Talk to me," Flash said into the intercom.

"Batman's found a match for the second DNA sample," Green Lantern reported. "He's traced it to a tiny island in the Pacific Ocean. It looks like the general is alive!"

The Flash's spirits soared, his hopes renewed.

"Meet me at the *Javelin-7,*" Green Lantern said. "We're going to pay the general a little visit."

"I can't leave Blaze," Flash replied, feeling reluctant to step away from her side.

"Flash, you can't help her here," Green Lantern shot back. "Finding Kolnikov is our only hope of saving her. She needs you, buddy."

"Go," Wonder Woman said, smiling. "I'll stay with her. If her condition changes, I will contact you, I promise."

Flash looked at Blaze. Her body trembled slightly; her face remained flushed.

"We're wasting time, folks!" Green Lantern shouted.

"I'm on my way," Flash replied. Then turning to Wonder Woman he added, "Thanks, Diana. I won't forget this."

As he sped from the med-lab, Flash paused for a fraction of a second to plant an unseen kiss on Blaze's cheek.

CHAPTER
12

Alexi Kolnikov stepped out onto the back deck of his one-story house, holding a cold glass of lemonade firmly in his left hand. He looked out at the ocean lapping gently at the powdery white sand. A warm breeze tousled his few remaining strands of gray hair.

The afternoon sun beat down on the small island nestled in the Pacific Ocean. Rows of tall palm trees lined the house, extending toward the sea. The house itself sat in the shadow of a long-dormant volcano that rose from the center of the island, then trailed away down a series of smaller mountain peaks. Lush gardens filled with exotic flowers and trees, and huge bountiful vegetables surrounded the house.

Kolnikov had planted these gardens himself. They

reminded him of the beautiful formal gardens at his home back in Russia. From time to time he missed them terribly. Digging in the dirt, however, helping to create natural beauty with his own hands, eased the longing he sometimes felt for his former country.

Settling into a chaise lounge, Kolnikov switched on his notebook computer and waited for his wireless Internet connection to kick in so he could check the day's news. Not that he was in any hurry. There was nowhere he had to go and no place he preferred to be more than this comfortable chaise on the deck of his home on this remote island.

As he waited for the connection to go through, Kolnikov once again thought back on the past twenty years of his life. He felt lucky and satisfied with the choices he had made, and he smiled at the thought of his former life as a top-ranking general in the former Soviet Union. Life here sometimes got lonely, but even at its worst, it was vastly preferable to the high-pressured, paranoid, cutthroat, and often deadly existence he had left behind. These days he tended his gardens and read a lot. He was, for the most part, a happy man.

His thoughts drifted back to his struggle with Dr. Pushkin and how he had overcome the scientist, shoving him into the cryogenic chamber. He flashed back on the slippery car ride away from the secret lab, driving Pushkin's car, which had then skidded off the road just as he leapt to safety. He recalled landing on the snow-covered road, then watching as the car tumbled over the cliff, exploding in a fireball below.

Kolnikov laughed softly to himself, recalling how the newspapers had reported Pushkin's death, assuming that his body had been reduced to ashes among the charred remains of his car.

And then, of course, he relived once more the event that had changed—and most probably saved—his life. After his encounter with Dr. Pushkin and his near-death experience on the road, he had begun to question his own commitment to the Soviets. To put so much into a project, only to be betrayed by his closest associate, had left him doubting his own motives and whether he could ever truly be a staunch nationalist again.

Then, not long after the incident in the cryogenic chamber, the extremely lucrative offer had arrived from a U.S. biotech firm willing to pay big bucks for secret Soviet genetic technology, which, of course, he had complete access to.

Kolnikov had taken the money, sold out his country, and vanished without a word, retiring to this tiny island paradise, where he had spent the last two decades in hiding, enjoying his life and marveling at the changes in the world.

Occasionally, but not too often, he thought about how different his life might have turned out had he turned down that offer. Mostly, he abandoned those thoughts, allowing them to drift away on the warm Pacific breezes.

A dull roar caught Kolnikov's attention, bringing his thoughts back to the present. The sound was faint at first, growing louder. Then a sleek silver aircraft came into view. It was not unusual for planes to fly by above the island. At least fifteen flights a day carrying tourists from California to Hawaii zoomed overhead. He had long ago learned to ignore them, not even hearing most of the air traffic that passed by at thirty-five thousand feet.

But this was different. The craft, which resembled a U.S. space shuttle more than any commercial jet-liner, was flying much lower than the usual air traffic. Placing his notebook down on the deck, Kolnikov rose from his chaise, following the aircraft's descent toward the island's single grass airstrip, where his private jet was kept.

The plane dropped from his view behind a line of palm trees. He could hear the craft's landing gear scrape against the ground and the whine of its engine soften, then go silent.

Sighing, he calmly returned to his chaise and sipped his drink. Apparently his years of solitude and privacy were about to come to an end.

The *Javelin-7* touched down, bouncing and shaking as it rolled to a stop on the narrow grass airstrip. The space-worthy vessel had not originally been designed to land on tiny, uneven runways such as this. But the Justice League used the sophisticated craft much like pilots flying small two-seater airplanes, landing the shuttle on rocky, rutted airstrips around the world.

Before the ship had come to a full stop, Flash had the cockpit canopy open and was scrambling out of the craft. Green Lantern followed.

"Okay, we're here," Flash said impatiently. "We know he's on this island. Now, how do we find this guy?"

"I'll do an aerial surveillance, you cover the ground on foot," Green Lantern suggested. "Stay in touch via comm link."

"Let's go," Flash replied, dashing off in a scarlet streak.

Green Lantern extended a green force field around himself, then sped into the air. A quick flight around the small island revealed only a handful of houses.

In a secluded spot, surrounded by trees, Green Lantern spotted a thin, mostly bald man stretched out on a chaise lounge on a deck. Aiming his data comm link toward the figure, he executed a quick DNA scan. It came up positive.

"Found him, hotshot," the Emerald Warrior reported over his comm link, transmitting the general's location to his partner. "Meet me at those coordinates." Then he swooped down from the sky, an emerald streak landing on the deck beside the horizontal figure. A few seconds later, Flash zoomed up beside him.

"General Kolnikov?" Green Lantern asked.

"My, my," the man replied, standing up. "No one has addressed me by my rank in many years. But, yes, I am Alexi Kolnikov, and at one time, about a million years ago, I did answer to 'General.' I certainly don't need to ask who you two are. Despite my isolation on this island, thanks to modern technology I am quite abreast of world events. I recognize Green Lantern and the Flash of the world-famous Justice League.

"And now, the obvious question. Why are you here, and how on Earth did you find me? But, I'm being rude. A glass of lemonade? I just mixed up a fresh pitcher."

"No thanks, General," Green Lantern replied. "We've got a problem."

As the Flash paced back and forth nervously, Green Lantern quickly filled Kolnikov in on their current situation, including the grim death of Dr. Pushkin.

"I was quite amused when I read about Red Dawn awakening after all these years, and about all the fuss they are causing at the World Assembly," Kolnikov revealed when Green Lantern had finished his tale. "They must have been quite surprised to find out that there is no more Cold War to fight."

"Some of them still don't believe that the Cold War ever ended," Green Lantern explained. "We were hoping to find you so that you could explain it to them. But now we have a more pressing problem. Do you know why the genetic integrity of Red Dawn is being compromised?"

"More important," Flash jumped in. "Do you know how to *fix* the problem?" He had practically exploded from impatience while Green Lantern told his tale.

Kolnikov sat back down and searched his mind. "It was all so long ago," he said. "But I do remember

Pushkin saying something about maintaining the integrity of their genetic structures."

"General Kolnikov!" a voice boomed from above.

The three men on the deck looked up to see Red Fury carrying Sinew. The two landed beside Kolnikov.

"It appears that everyone has found me," Kolnikov said. "Red Fury, Sinew, it is good to see you. I have heard of your awakening and your current troubles."

"Don't believe their lies," Red Fury shouted.

"They are telling the truth, my friend," Kolnikov replied. "The Cold War is indeed over. Your original purpose no longer has any meaning in this new world. The Soviet Union collapsed, it was not conquered. And yes, we are now friends with the United States and our other allies in the West. But today's Russia needs heroes more than ever. Red Dawn can still serve a valuable purpose in this world."

"Why should we believe you, General?" Red Fury shouted, looking around at the house and gardens. "How did you acquire the means to live your very comfortable, secluded life here?"

"I admit that back then I did some things the Soviet government would not have approved of," Kolnikov said. "Maybe sold a secret or two. But that's ancient history now."

"So you admit to being a traitor, and then you ask me to believe you," Red Fury blustered. "No!"

"Listen," Flash said, running out of patience. "You've got a much bigger problem. Have you forgotten? You're going to die, unless he can remember what Pushkin said twenty years ago."

"The stabilizing field!" Kolnikov shouted. "That's it! I remember now. Red Dawn was exposed to a stabilizing field right before the freezing process took place. But Pushkin said that they had to be exposed to the same stabilizing field soon after awakening, as well, in order to maintain the integrity of their genetic structures! That must be why Pushkin didn't live long after awakening. He was never exposed to the stabilizing field, either before or after being placed in hibernation."

"Let's go!" Flash cried. "We've got to get Blaze back to that lab and expose her to the stabilizing field again! You two are welcome to come if—"

When Flash turned toward the spot where Red Fury and Sinew had been standing, he found that they were gone.

"Apparently those two are incapable of trusting me," said Kolnikov, pointing after Red Fury and Sinew, who had flown to the top of the nearby volcano. "Even at the price of their own lives."

Red Fury stood on a thin ledge at the top of the long-inactive volcano, with Sinew at his side. So great was his anger at General Kolnikov's apparent betrayal, the leader of Red Dawn hadn't stuck around long enough to discover that the general indeed had the one piece of information that could save his life.

"We may die, Sinew," Red Fury snarled. "But so will the general!"

Sinew had never seen her comrade so enraged, so completely out of control. Even she, who had been his most loyal partner, began to question both his sanity and the wisdom of his current course of action.

Peering deep into the opening at the top of the mountain, Red Fury fired twin beams of intense heat into the volcano.

A deep rumble shook the island.

"We don't have time for this!" Flash cried. "We've got to get back."

"I'm afraid not, hotshot," Green Lantern said as the rumbling grew louder and steam poured from the volcano's top. "It looks like Red Fury has activated that volcano with his heat beams. If that thing blows, it'll wipe out not only Kolnikov, but everyone else on this island."

At that moment, the volcano spat forth a small flow

of lava. The flaming liquid rock dripped down the side of the mountain, a preview of more intense destruction to follow.

Up on the edge of the volcano, Red Fury and Sinew peered down into the fiercely bubbling lava.

"The traitor will pay dearly for his treachery," Red Fury exclaimed. Then a wave of dizziness overcame him, much more intense than the sensation he had first felt during his battle with Wonder Woman. Sweat broke out on his face as his legs gave way, no longer able to support his body. He let out a shriek of pain and collapsed, tumbling into the churning volcano.

"No!" cried Sinew. She dove toward him, her right arm outstretched over the edge, reaching down and closing her fist on what she hoped would be Red Fury's arm. But she was too late and now clutched at the air, empty-handed.

Seeing Red Fury vanish below the lip of the volcano, Flash reacted instinctively, speeding up the side of the mountain, past the spot where Sinew lay sprawled, then down inside the volcano's outer wall.

He reached a point just above the scorching lava, then extended his arms and caught Red Fury's plunging body mere seconds before it would have splashed into the molten rock.

"Gotcha!" Flash cried as his left foot narrowly skimmed the surface of the blistering magma.

Finding his footing on a thin ledge just above the lava, the Flash strained under the heft of Red Fury's considerable weight. Fighting to keep his balance, Flash dashed along the inner rim of the mountain.

"Yow!" he cried, feeling intense heat seep through his costume. His skin burned and his legs ached from the extra effort of thrusting his body forward while supporting his hefty burden.

Flash finally reached the far side of the volcano. He ran up the inner wall, over the outer lip, then down the far side of the mountain. Reaching Green Lantern and General Kolnikov, the Scarlet Speedster placed Red Fury's unconscious body onto the ground.

"I think he's alive," Flash said, gasping, winded from his rescue effort. "But if you'll excuse me . . ."

Foosh!

Flash raced across the tiny island, back past the grass airstrip, heading toward the ocean. He dashed across the white sand beach, then dove headfirst into the breakers, submerging his body completely in the cool water.

Relief came instantly. As he cooled, feeling returned to his numb, blistered feet. *Note to self,* he thought as he stepped from the water. *The next time you go volcano-hopping, wear very, very thick-soled boots, and try not to be carrying an extra 250 pounds of muscle!*

By the time Flash had run back to the others, his costume had dried completely, the wind created by his superspeed having evaporated the water as he moved.

"You okay, hotshot?" Green Lantern asked.

"Fine," Flash replied. "I just thought it would be a nice time for a little dip in the ocean." Looking down at the soles of his boots, he saw that they were black and shredded. "My shoes could use a shine, though. How's he?" he asked, nodding toward Red Fury.

"Not so good," Green Lantern replied. "We can't bring him around, and his whole body keeps shaking."

"Come on, you big, stubborn lug," Flash said, kneeling beside the sweating, twitching figure on the ground. "I didn't almost turn my feet into toast just to have you die!"

"You saved him," said a low, strained voice from behind.

Whirling around, Flash saw Sinew standing a few yards away.

"You risked your life to save your enemy," she said in amazement.

"Like I've been saying about ten billion times," Flash replied, turning back to Red Fury. "We are not your enemy."

"I know that now," Sinew said. "But I fear that we have learned it too late."

"We've got to get both of you back to the lab," Flash said, leaping to his feet. "We'll have to pick up Blaze and—"

"Ahhhhh!"

Red Fury's scream startled everyone. They watched in horror as his face began to stretch and his skin split, dropping away in jagged, bleeding clumps.

Sinew stared down in horror and Flash looked away bitterly as the life drained from Red Fury's body, his blood spreading in the milky-white sand. Within minutes the process was over. A small pool of liquid genetic material mingled with the red and green costume of the former leader of project Red Dawn.

Flash was stunned by the depth of his sadness for the loss of a so-called enemy. "I thought I had saved him," he said bitterly.

"You did all you could, Flash," Green Lantern replied, clasping a firm but comforting hand on Flash's shoulder. "Right now, we've got to help the others."

Blaze! The single word filled Flash's thoughts. "Let's go!"

SPLOOM! VOOOSH!

Plumes of lava shot from the volcano, splattering and sizzling down the sides of the mountain.

"It appears that Red Fury may have the last laugh on us, after all," Kolnikov said, watching as flames and smoke poured from the volcano.

"No!" shouted Sinew. "He was wrong, General. I know that now. And I will not let destruction be his legacy."

Running with surprising speed, Sinew dashed back toward the volcano. She felt foolish having held on to her outdated beliefs for so long. Still, she could not bring herself to be disloyal to Red Fury. With her leader gone, she felt the need to make up for his final mistake.

Sinew reached the top of a smaller mountain adjacent to the volcano. The mountain's peak came to a fairly sharp point tapering down to a narrow ledge on all sides. Moving swiftly around the thin strip of rock, Sinew unleashed earth-shattering punches. Her fists plunged deep into the mountain, blasting large holes all the way around.

When she had completed perforating the top section of the mountain, she shoved her hands into two of the holes and lifted. Straining to the very limits of her enormous strength, Sinew tore the top off the mountain, struggling to keep her balance as she supported the round, conelike chunk of rock.

"Let me give you a hand with that," said a voice from above.

Green Lantern hovered in midair. Aiming his power ring, the Emerald Warrior surrounded the chunk of mountaintop with a wide beam. Then he lifted the cone-shaped rock from Sinew's grasp, rotating it so that the sharp point now faced downward.

Guiding the rock over the still-spewing volcano, Green Lantern lowered it into the opening, then released his power beam.

FUMP!

The enormous chunk of mountaintop slammed into the volcano's gaping mouth. While not a perfect fit, it did the job of capping the churning lava, keeping it contained within the mountain, allowing enough steam to escape so that pressure didn't build up beneath it. The lava would eventually cool down and the volcano would resume its dormant state.

Green Lantern landed next to Sinew on the ledge of the nearby mountain. "Good idea," he said, extending his hand.

"Thank you for your assistance," she replied, reaching out and accepting the handshake. "I thought I could carry that piece of the mountain over to the volcano myself, but I suppose there are limits even to my great strength."

"That's why we work as a team," Green Lantern said.

"I look forward to working with you again," Sinew offered.

Then she collapsed into the Emerald Warrior's arms.

Red light pulsated, filling the central room of the cryogenic laboratory deep in the Ural Mountains. Four figures lay motionless, strapped onto lab tables, as the crimson energy washed over them.

In the lab's control room, Flash paced back and forth anxiously. Wonder Woman followed him from one end of the room to the other, trying to help steady his nerves. Green Lantern sat at the main computer, supervising the operation. With Batman's assistance via the comm link, he had managed to set up the stabilizing field that now surrounded the four surviving members of Red Dawn.

Flash and Green Lantern had taken Sinew to the *Javelin-7*. After a brief stop at the Watchtower to pick up Blaze and Wonder Woman, they had headed back to the lab in Russia. Beacon and Gray Heron were already sprawled on the lab tables, near death. As Batman and Green Lantern had accessed the computer sequence to engage the stabilizing field, Flash and Wonder Woman had strapped Blaze and Sinew down for the procedure.

The heroes had also agreed to keep General Kolnikov's whereabouts secret from the Russian authorities. Those officials who may have heard of the general most likely assumed he was dead. Kolnikov was happy in his life away from the rest of the world. Flash and Green Lantern saw no reason to disturb that privacy, especially since the information he had provided gave Red Dawn their one chance for survival.

The stabilizing process wound down, and the bright red glow faded slowly, replaced by the faint illumination of dim white lights. Restraining straps retracted, and the four figures stirred, drifting gradually back to consciousness.

One by one they slid from the tables, confused, but relieved to be alive.

Flash couldn't stand it any longer. He zoomed to Blaze's side.

"Wanna race?" he joked, watching as her strength returned with each passing second.

"Give me ten minutes," she replied, rubbing her temples. "Then I'll give you a head start."

"Cute," said Flash, greatly relieved. "I'm glad you're feeling better."

"Thank you all," Sinew said as Green Lantern and Wonder Woman joined the others in the central room. "You have saved our lives."

"Where is Red Fury?" Beacon asked as his head began to clear.

Sinew filled him and Gray Heron in on the events that had taken place on the volcanic island.

"We were foolish to follow him so blindly," Gray Heron said, spreading his wings for the first time since falling ill. "I had a strong sense that he was wrong. But I chose to ignore it."

"Loyalty is an admirable trait," Green Lantern replied. "But you've got to trust your own judgment as well."

"So what do we do now?" Blaze asked.

"I'd love to show you around the USA, my home, sweet home," Flash replied quickly.

"I meant about our futures," Blaze explained, gesturing toward her three teammates.

"I think your great powers could be put to use helping the Russian people," Green Lantern said. "Not to mention the rest of the world. You might have been created to be weapons of war, but there's plenty of work for you to do right here, even with the Cold War over. The Justice League would be happy to contact the Russian authorities and set up the introductions."

"Yes," Sinew said, with Beacon and Gray Heron nodding their agreement. "We can be of use to our people. And maybe one day Russia will speak of Red Dawn the way the world now views the heroes of the Justice League."

"I look forward to that day," Green Lantern said.

"I'd still like to show you around," Flash offered Blaze, once again reluctant to leave, having come so close to losing her.

Blaze nodded. "I would like that," she said. "I would like that very much."

EPILOGUE

Flash and his teammates gathered on the Watchtower. Blaze had decided to stay in Russia for a few days to help the other members of Red Dawn adjust. She would then rejoin Flash in Central City for a couple of days before returning home for good.

Superman, J'onn J'onzz, and Hawkgirl had returned from the World Assembly, where tensions between the United States and Russia had eased. Russian authorities were filled in on the details of Red Dawn and a meeting was set up so that they could officially meet their very own team of super heroes.

"And so, Flash?" J'onn J'onzz asked. "Are you ready for another lesson in meditation?"

"Nah," the Scarlet Speedster replied, his thoughts

focused on Blaze's return. "I understand how important it is for me to slow down and appreciate what really matters. But for the moment, at least, things seem to be moving at just the right pace."

"Tell me about this Bond person again," Blaze said, shoving a fistful of popcorn into her mouth.

"Bond. James Bond," Flash replied, reaching over and scooping out some for himself from the large round tub that Blaze clutched in her arms. "He's a superspy, he saves the world, he fought the Russians . . . all right, not funny!"

Blaze rolled her eyes and reached for the large container of soda resting in the built-in cup holder on the back of the seat in front of her. She took a long, sweet sip.

The crowd filed into the Central City Multiplex, finding seats, carrying their munchies.

"The popcorn and soda are enough," Blaze said. "The movie feels like a bonus."

"And there's more," Flash replied, grabbing another handful of popcorn. "After the movie, we'll get some iced mocha. Then for tomorrow, I got tickets to the Central City 400. It's a stock car race. It's fast. Not as fast as us, but it's very cool. You'll love it!"

Sitting in the movie theater in Central City, Blaze felt pleased with her decision to visit Flash in the United States. So far, he had taken her to an amusement park, a miniature golf course, a bowling alley, two malls, an art museum, and a concert at a local club.

She was enjoying her whirlwind tour of the American cultural landscape, but her thoughts had started to turn toward the meeting scheduled to take place in a few days back home. Red Dawn was to be formally introduced to Russia's highest governmental and military officials, and Blaze was anxious, but also excited, to start her new life as a hero in her own land.

She felt a great responsibility to her teammates, who were really her only family, and she hoped that one day soon Red Dawn and the Justice League would team up to help the world. Blaze had also grown quite fond of Flash, and knew she would miss him when she left in a few days. But thanks to their superspeed, she felt confident that their blossoming transcontinental friendship would be easy enough to maintain.

As the lights in the theater dimmed and the first

commercial flickered up onto the screen, she turned and kissed Flash softly on the cheek. "Thank you," she whispered. "For everything."

"Sweetheart," he said, looking right at her. "I think this is the beginning of a beautiful friendship."

ABOUT THE AUTHOR

MICHAEL TEITELBAUM is the author of *Justice League: Secret Origins* (Bantam Books). He has been a writer, editor, and packager of children's books, comic books, and magazines for more than twenty years. He has worked on staff as an editor at Gold Key Comics, Golden Books, Putnam/Grosset, and Macmillan. His packaging company, Town Brook Press, created and packaged *Spider-Man Magazine*, a monthly publication, for Marvel Entertainment. Michael Teitelbaum's more recent writing includes the Garfield: Pet Force books (a series of five titles); *Breaking Barriers: In Sports, In Life* (based on the life of Jackie Robinson); *Samurai Jack: The Legend Begins*; and *Batman Beyond: Return of the Joker* (all published by Scholastic); junior novels based on the feature films *Men in Black II* and *Spider-Man* (HarperCollins); and *Smallville: Arrival* (Little, Brown). Michael and his wife, Sheleigah, split their time between New York City and their 160-year-old farmhouse in upstate New York.